THE IMAGE
OF A DRAWN SWORD

By the same author

NOVELS

The Scapegoat
The Wonderful Summer
The Passing of a Hero
Private View
Conventional Weapons
The Orchid Trilogy (*The Military Orchid*,
A Mine of Serpents, The Goose Cathedral)

AUTOBIOGRAPHICAL

The Dog at Clambercrown

POEMS

December Spring
The Elements of Death

BOTANY

The Wild Orchids of Britain
The Flowers in Season

SURREALISM

The Crisis in Bulgaria (pictures)

EDITED

The Denton Welch Journals

THE IMAGE
OF
A DRAWN SWORD

Jocelyn Brooke

INTRODUCTION BY
ANTHONY POWELL

SECKER & WARBURG
LONDON

First published in England 1950 by
John Lane The Bodley Head Limited.
This edition published in England 1982
by Martin Secker & Warburg Limited,
54 Poland Street, London W1V 3DF.

Introduction copyright © Anthony Powell 1982

British Library Cataloguing in Publication Data

Brooke, Jocelyn
    The image of a drawn sword.
    I. Title
    823'.914[F]   PR6052.R58127

    ISBN 0-436-06951-2

Photoset by
Rowland Phototypesetting Limited, Bury St Edmunds, Suffolk
Printed in Great Britain by
St Edmundsbury Press, Bury St Edmunds, Suffolk

TO THE MEMORY OF
Captain Cecil Henry Martin Brooke
The Buffs

Nu is se raed gelang
Eft oet the anum. Eard git ne const,
Frecne stowe, thaer thu findan miht
Felasinnigne secg: sec gif thu dyrre!

Beowulf

Contents

	Introduction *by Anthony Powell*	9
ONE	His Totem, the Fox	13
TWO	Parted in the Middle	16
THREE	Not Marked on the Ordnance Map	24
FOUR	Like Blown Leaves	30
FIVE	Between Sea and Sky	34
SIX	A Dual Image	42
SEVEN	Eligible for Enlistment	50
EIGHT	The Darkening Land	57
NINE	Like Some Unhappy Ghost	61
TEN	A Queer Caper	65
ELEVEN	The First of December	71
TWELVE	The Patch of Alexanders	80
THIRTEEN	Buds of Lent-Lilies	84
FOURTEEN	Stripped for a Fight	94
FIFTEEN	The Image of a Drawn Sword	103
SIXTEEN	Tassels of Woodspurge	114
SEVENTEEN	The Roman Camp	120
EIGHTEEN	In Some Other World	127
NINETEEN	A Fight to the Death	134
TWENTY	The Living Moment	138

Introduction

Not many of Jocelyn Brooke's readers are likely to translate for themselves on sight the epigraph from *Beowulf* which ushers in *The Image of a Drawn Sword*. The quotation (its Old English said to be slightly mistranscribed) is at once impish and serious, a typical piece of Brooke fancy; Anglo-Saxon, for the type of Oxford undergraduate Brooke elsewhere represents himself, being usually looked on as the unavoidable drawback – not to say crucifixion – of the English School.

Nonetheless the 10th-century poem's brooding sinister horror, which even the most anti-*Beowulf* student could scarcely deny, must have struck a chord when Brooke examined his own daydreams. I am told the lines read: 'Now once again counsel is in your power alone. You do not know the place, the terrible area, where you could find the much-sinning creature. Seek it if you dare!'

These words are spoken to the hero, Beowulf, by Hrothgar, king of the Danes, after the monster Grendel's mother – herself equally monstrous – has come to the great hall of Heorot and killed Aeschere, Hrothgar's closest friend.

In an introduction to Jocelyn Brooke's three volumes of lightly fictionalized autobiography, *The Orchid Trilogy* (1981), I noted that although action in *The Image of a Drawn Sword* takes place in Brooke's familiar Kentish landscape (place-names like Clambercrown the same as those of the trilogy) the book can unquestionably be categorized as a novel; yet 'even here a form of autobiography is not entirely lacking, because in place of Brooke's physical experience, a kind of vision of the phantasies that sometimes haunted his mind is set out, especially phantasies about the army.'

The last aspect should have been expressed more strongly. In spite of *The Image* being undeniably a novel it is in at least one respect Brooke's most autobiographical work; that is to say in the manner he chronicles what was going on within himself below the surface: sadomasochist imaginings; homosexual desires; sentiments towards his mother; worries about a career; sense of guilt as to want of will-power. This last element particularly makes itself felt. The others are there too in one form or another.

The name of Kafka has often been invoked to describe the genre of *The Image*, the qualities of which might be judged little if at all inferior to the supposed model. Brooke told me that he had in fact never read any Kafka when he wrote the book. I believe him. It has, however, been pointed out that in *The Military Orchid* (1948), opening volume of the trilogy, the sentence occurs: 'a curious paranoid quality, like a story by Kafka.' *The Image* was first published in 1950.

There are two possibilities: either Brooke wrote *The Image* before *The Military Orchid*, or – like many another – he took Kafka's name in vain without having read him. Brooke would have been the first to laugh at being convicted of such intellectual pretension at a period when so thick and fast fell the Kafka-addicts, that I remember expressing hope as a reviewer that a time would come when it would be possible to write:

It was a summer evening,
Old Kafka's work was done.

I feel fairly sure that the first answer is the true one: that Brooke wrote *The Image* before *The Military Orchid*. The unusual course taken by Brooke's literary progress explains why such an uncertainty can exist.

After service in the ranks of the Royal Army Medical Corps during the second war he re-enlisted in the RAMC a year or two after demobilization. He was nearly forty when he began to produce a steady flow of books (sometimes two or more a year) after deciding to 'buy himself out' of the army.

It seems reasonable to suppose that Brooke had at least made extensive notes about some of his projected writings before they appeared. He may even have completed *The Image*, anyway more or less, in the interlude between coming out of the army and rejoining. Its theme undoubtedly embodies inner torments gone through in deciding whether or not to take that step, though perhaps it was completed on return to comparative tranquillity.

There are several reasons for supposing Brooke wrote *The Image* first, but considered *The Military Orchid* a better opening card. For instance the autobiographical *persona* which runs through all the rest of Jocelyn Brooke's works has not yet been fully developed; the phrasing too is at times less assured than it was to become. There may be resemblances to Brooke in Reynard Langrish, who lives in a cottage with his widowed mother, was invalided during the war, works in a bank, but he is a far less sardonic figure than the narrator of the later first-person books.

Between Reynard and Roy Archer, the young regular officer who comes to the cottage after losing his way, in due course persuading Reynard to undertake some sort of military training owing to a threatened 'emergency', there is a suggestion of mutual homosexual attraction. This is conveyed without undue emphasis or the touch of satire which usually accompanies Brooke's subsequent treatment of such relationships.

An unfathomable nightmare for Reynard now begins, in which he agrees to undertake at least some of the training that Archer puts forward as a duty, while Reynard, on his side, always stops short of actual military engagement. The local army authorities, on the other hand (so far as they can be identified by Reynard) increasingly regard him as committed. In consequence of this he finally finds himself under arrest for desertion.

Now disaster falls. Brooke's story is full of suspense, and it would be inappropriate here to give too much indication of what happens. Indeed, what does happen is not at all certain. Brooke is dextrous at mixing reality with phantasy, recording the quick shifts of time in which the tensions that beset Reynard are suddenly redoubled.

From the moment at the beginning of the book when mysterious bugle-calls sound in the distance, although no barracks are situated in the neighbourhood of the cottage, to that when Reynard actually takes part with other recruits in physical training on the site of the former Roman Camp, the reader is never sure whether or not such things are conceived only in Reynard's disturbed imagination; self-dramatizations that have no basis in fact.

The blue and red serpent curling round a sword that is tattooed on the arm of Reynard's fellow recruits (which seems to be memory of a Divisional shoulder flash during the war) also appears on the arm of a tramp Reynard falls in with near the Roman Camp, by then deserted. It might also be worth noting that in the collection of Welsh tales known as *The Mabinogion* (tr. Gwyn Jones), medieval though dating back to a much earlier period, the story called *The*

Dream of Rhonabwy has the following passage: 'Lo, he arising, and Arthur's sword in his hand, and the image of two serpents on the sword in gold: and when the sword was drawn from its sheath as it were two flames of fire might be seen from the mouths of the serpents, and so exceeding dreadful was it that it was not easy for any to look thereon.' Could it be that Brooke deliberately brought together Anglo-Saxon and Brito-Celtic myth?

Roy Archer comes from time to time to the bank to cash a cheque, but takes no notice of Reynard working behind the counter. Reynard's mother never seems at all disturbed when her son fears that military involvements have caused him to come home unwontedly late. Is all this merely the condition of being a 'loner' in an unusually neurotic condition? If so, that state is wonderfully well portrayed.

The climax of *The Image of a Drawn Sword*, the fate of Reynard's mother and her cottage, the circumstances of the violent death of his love, his own calm walk towards what must also be death, all lead back to the *Beowulf* epigraph, still obscure in complicating further already complex symbols, yet nevertheless illustrating in a novel of horrifying intensity 'the counsel that is in his power alone' and 'the terrible area' named by Hrothgar.

ANTHONY POWELL

CHAPTER ONE

His Totem, the Fox

The autumnal dusk was thickening across the valley as Reynard Langrish jumped off the bus from Glamber and began to walk down the lane towards the village. The lane was bordered on one side by a plantation of beeches, between whose straight, slender boles the sunset sky gleamed with a watery brightness; on the other side fields sloped gently down to the valley where, muffled among trees, the village showed indeterminately, hazed with the river mists.

Across the valley, raised slightly above the level of the other houses, a lighted window shone brightly through the gathering dusk. Reynard observed it with satisfaction, aware that his mother would already be preparing tea and that, in another ten minutes, he himself would enter the sitting-room and be once again absorbed into the placid, fire-lapped comfort of his home. Yet his satisfaction was mitigated by a half-conscious awareness of its falsity; his anxiety to reach home was largely a matter of habit, surviving from an earlier and happier period. Hurrying homeward now, a vague, unwitting reluctance seized upon him and, half-way down the lane, he paused and leaned against a gate leading into the fields. Without wholly admitting it to himself, he had come, lately, to feel an inexplicable dread of his daily homecoming. Before he had been in the house ten minutes, he knew that he would begin to chafe at his mother's presence, at the warm, confined ambience of the living-room, the familiar objects ranged unalterably in their places. Sooner or later, during the course of the evening, he would be compelled to escape from the house, to walk aimlessly along the deserted lanes and cart-tracks, possessed by a restless craving to be above and beyond the sight and hearing of his home.

At the bank in Glamber where he worked, the daily routine inhibited this restlessness; he became fully aware of it only in the evenings. Leaning, now, against the gate into the fields, it seemed to him that the very countryside itself was exerting upon him an invisible, indefinable pressure, producing, in his fatigued brain, an intolerable sense of confinement. At the same time, the features of the landscape took on a peculiar appearance of unreality, as though seen through a distorting lens, or reproduced by some inferior photographic process.

The sensation, unpleasant as it was, caused him no surprise; for some weeks past he had suffered from this disquieting sense of 'unreality', and he had already, to some extent, come to terms with it. It was as though he were living under a glass bell, through which he was able to perceive the normal features of the world, but which prohibited him from any direct contact with it. The illusion was strengthened by an actual degeneration, slight but unmistakable, in his sensory perceptions; his sense of smell had become defective – perhaps due to a chronic catarrh – and his hearing, too, was slightly impaired. Accustomed to ill health in recent years (he had been invalided out of the Army during the war, after an attack of rheumatic fever) he had not so far troubled to consult a doctor; there seemed, indeed, no particular reason why he should do so – his symptoms amounted to little more than a feeling of being 'off colour'; yet he was, in fact, more worried about the state of his health than he liked to admit.

He fixed his eyes now upon the ground near his feet, where, in the thickening dusk, he could just detect a clump of Herb-Robert, its delicate pink blossoms vaguely defined against the darker mass of leaves. The plant, so familiar, rooted with so natural a grace in the hedge-bank, gave him a certain fleeting solace. As though to confirm his relationship with the exterior world, he pulled out a cigarette and lit it; but the cigarette was tasteless – it was some time now since he had been able to enjoy the flavour of tobacco – and the habitual motions of smoking seemed curiously unreal, as though he were watching somebody performing the action in a jerky, old-fashioned film.

He raised his eyes once again to the lighted window across the valley; but the last vestiges of his pleasure in the sight had drained away from him, he was aware now only of the intolerable sense of captivity which awaited him in the warm, fire-lit room.

Abruptly, he flung the tasteless cigarette away, watching it strike the road with a little sputter of sparks. Then, disconsolately, he continued his walk down the hill. As he neared the village, a labourer shuffled by in the half-darkness, and greeted him as he passed:

'Evening, Mr Reynard!'

The use of the Christian name gave him a sudden, ingenuous pleasure, reminding him that he, a bank-clerk, belonged to this countryside, was united to it, even, by the vestiges of a relationship which could almost be termed feudal. Langrishes had owned land here for centuries; his own great-uncle (from whom he inherited the name of Reynard) had lived in the manor-house; within two generations the family had become dispersed – the land was sold up, the sons had gone into business or the Service – but among the older cottagers the feudal tradition survived.

Reynard stepped out with a sudden briskness, feeling an un-accustomed pride in his forebears, and in the curious name which had descended to him from the last owner of the manor. Reynard – it was the badge of his cunning, a totem-symbol, strengthening him in his guerrilla war against the powers which oppressed him. He crossed the village street, and walked on towards his home with a new confidence – secure in the guardianship of his totem, the fox.

CHAPTER TWO

Parted in the Middle

As he approached his home, the darkness deepened rapidly: a heavy mass of cloud had swept up to the zenith, and large drops of rain began to fall, driving obliquely against his face in the rising south-west wind. In a few moments the wind seemed to reach gale force, tearing through the great chestnuts by the church so that their ancient branches creaked perilously overhead as Reynard passed beneath them. By the time he reached the house it was raining heavily. He pushed open the door and stepped into the warm-lit room; his mother, grey-haired and placid, raised her head, and he leaned over and kissed her without speaking, as was his habit; for Mrs Langrish had for many years now been completely and incurably deaf.

Calmly, she continued to make preparations for the evening meal: laying out the cold meat, the tea-things, the cutlery, with a deft and silent concentration of purpose. Reynard flung himself into a chair and picked up the day's paper, his eyes running vaguely over the headlines, scarcely aware of the significance of what he read. The reading of a newspaper had become for him lately an almost intolerable effort; periodically, ashamed of his profound ignorance of current affairs, he would make good resolutions and read *The Times* from cover to cover: yet an hour afterwards he could hardly have repeated a single item of news. Nor did the house possess a wireless-set, for Mrs Langrish, in her deafness, found the electrical vibrations in some way painful, and Reynard had been only too willing to deprive himself of anything which marred her comfort; wishing only, indeed, that he were able to do more for her in her affliction.

Putting aside the paper, he glanced aimlessly about the room, noting once again the too-familiar objects ranged with precision in their accustomed places; the Angelica Kaufmann engravings, the Benares brass-ware, the photograph of his father in full-dress uniform. . . . With a flicker of interest, he noted one slight change since the previous evening: a beaten-copper pot, which had previously contained Michaelmas daisies, now held a tall, spreading cluster of spindle-berries. In the soft light, the berries glowed with a peculiar intensity, as though illumined from within. Mrs Langrish, seeing her son's eyes resting upon them, made an obscure, explanatory gesture and smiled briefly.

'John Quested brought them in,' she remarked.

Presently mother and son sat down in silence to their meal. The wind raged with an increasing violence round the house, and rain spattered viciously against the windows. Before the end of the meal, Reynard felt unbearably restless; aware that it would be foolish to take his usual evening walk in such weather, yet determined, none the less, to escape as soon as possible from the too comfortable room and from the constraint of his mother's presence. Mrs Langrish, however, ate slowly; and common courtesy demanded that her son should at least wait till she had finished. No sooner had she swallowed her last mouthful, than he began impatiently to clear the table; by the time she herself reached the kitchen, he was already half-way through the washing-up. He completed the task rapidly, signing to her to return to the sitting-room. Following her soon after, he crossed from habit to the piano, sat down, and began at once to play, rather mechanically and without much expression, a Mozart sonata.

Confined within the prison of her deafness, his mother was yet able to watch, with an expert eye, the motions of his fingers. A proficient pianist herself in past days, she would even on occasion criticize his technique, suggesting that a certain passage should be taken more *legato*, or that his tempo was at fault. To-night, however, she watched his performance in unbroken silence. Soon he tired of the music, and returned to his chair by the fireside.

With the physical relaxation, he was aware once again, disquietingly, of the sense of 'unreality' which he had experienced during his walk home; an Indian bowl, his father's photograph, the spindle-berries, seemed to tremble like a mirage upon the verge of dissolution; it was as though his personality – or the sensory images which gave it form and solidity – were undergoing some process of disintegration, as though the several parts of himself lay scattered about the perimeter of a gradually widening circle. . . . It seemed to him, moreover (as it had seemed on more than one occasion lately), that unless he made a prodigious effort to draw back within himself these *disjecta membra*, he would find, too late, that the process had gone beyond his control. . . . More than once, too, it had occurred to him to wonder if, after all, his efforts were worth while: was this precious 'identity', to which he found himself so tenaciously clinging, of such supreme value after all?

From habit, he found himself concentrating upon the first object which offered itself to his lazy and unselective vision. On the present occasion, this happened to be the faded image of his father, cheaply framed in *passe-partout*. He noted, indolently, the drooping Edwardian moustache, the jutting chin, the hand clasping the sword-hilt. . . .

Suddenly, with a clamour that made him spring to his feet, the noise of the front-door bell pealed through the house. Unprecedented at such an hour, and on such a night, the sound penetrated even to the consciousness of Mrs Langrish – or so it seemed to Reynard, though possibly it was his own startled movement that had caught her attention; in either case, her placid face took on a mobility of expression such as it had not displayed throughout the evening. For a moment, mother and son faced one another, their eyes meeting in a sudden communion of shared apprehension. Reynard continued to stand for several seconds, stock still beneath his father's photograph; he felt an unaccountable temptation to ignore the summons completely, to pretend to his mother that he had started at some imaginary noise. In the same instant he was stricken, more acutely than ever before, with the sense of some vast impending dissolution: it was as though, within his brain, some seismic disturbance was taking place, some revolution of natural forces which he was powerless to resist.

Unsteadily, as though the very ground were heaving beneath him, he moved to the hallway, switching on the light as he did so. As he crossed the hall, the bell pealed once more, and to its clamour was added a thunderous knocking. Trembling, as if the action were fraught with some immense and world-shaking significance, he lifted the latch of the front door. . . .

Immediately he staggered backwards, with difficulty preventing himself from falling. At the moment of his lifting the latch, a particularly violent gust of wind had hurled itself against the house, and the door, facing its full blast, had swung open with irresistible force. So powerful was the inrush of air that a vase of dahlias on the hall table crashed to the ground, and a straw mat rose from the floor as though possessed of a daemonic life of its own.

The light streamed out through the open doorway, kindling to a sudden brilliance the sharp, slanting needles of the rain. Against this bright, metallic curtain stood the tall figure of a young man: framed in the narrow doorway, he seemed immense, larger than life – a visionary being conjured out of the night's wildness. His light-coloured belted mackintosh gleamed with wetness, beads of rain sparkled like diamonds in his blond hair, his cheeks glowed with the vivid, rain-washed brilliance of autumn berries.

For several moments the two men stood staring at one another, wordlessly. Then, taking sudden command of himself, Reynard took a step backward.

'Come in out of the rain,' he said.

The stranger proved, after all, to be no daemonic vision, but a perfectly ordinary young man. Yet his first impression lingered oddly in Reynard's mind, and he was aware of a curious sense of exaltation, mingled with a vague, unformulated fear. This man, he thought, was one who held authority; what kind of authority he could not guess, but he was none the less convinced of the truth of his impression.

The man stepped forward.

'I say, I'm frightfully sorry,' he stammered, his lips parting in an amiable smile. 'I'm afraid I've lost my way.'

Once again Reynard met his eyes: gleaming with an extraordinary depth and brilliance, they seemed to reflect all the wild darkness and wetness of the night.

'Fact is, I've got a car outside,' the visitor was saying. 'I was on my way over from Glamber, but I had to go and see a chap up at Stelling Minnis, and I seem to have missed my road. D'you know the old "Dog" at Clambercrown? I must have taken the wrong turning at the cross-roads there. . . . I'm on my way to Larchester, actually – got to be there by half-past eight.'

'You've plenty of time,' Reynard assured him, his voice sounding a trifle unsteady. 'Come in.'

'But look here, I'm awfully sorry to knock you up like this. . . . Fact is, yours seemed to be the only light hereabouts – they must go to bed early in this place. What's the name of it, by the by?'

'This is Priorsholt. You're only about three miles from Larchester – I can put you on the road. There's no difficulty, once you know it. Come in and get warm for a moment.'

'Honestly, I don't think I ought to. . . .'

'Yes, do.' Reynard spoke with an insistence which surprised himself. Suddenly it seemed important that he should make the stranger's acquaintance. 'I should take your mac off,' he added, hospitably.

He helped the young man off with his drenched mackintosh, and again, for an instant, their eyes met. Simultaneously, a spark of recognition sprang between then.

'Surely, you're Mr—I mean, Captain Archer,' Reynard exclaimed, haltingly.

'Yes, Archer's my name – Roy Archer. I've seen you somewhere, but I can't think quite where. . . .'

'I work in the United Midland at Glamber,' Reynard explained.

'Of course – I knew your face directly you opened the door. Don't know your name, I'm afraid.'

Reynard supplied it.

'Oh, yes – Langrish,' the other murmured, eyeing Reynard with a curiously searching expression. His next words were so unexpected that Reynard fancied he must have misheard them: 'I was expecting to run into you sometime.'

'Expecting — ?' Reynard echoed, with surprise.

'Oh, well, you know. . . .' Archer's voice was suddenly vague; he gave a soft, friendly chuckle. 'You never know, do you?' he added, rather fatuously. But Reynard had detected a peculiar look of embarrassment in his eyes, as though his words had been spoken unwittingly.

Reynard led the way into the sitting-room, and rapidly explained to his mother, in the low-pitched tones which she found most easily intelligible, what had happened. Introductions were performed: Roy Archer greeted his hostess with tact and self-possession, but Mrs Langrish, with the unpredictableness of the very deaf, had relapsed into one of those moods in which she seemed more cut off than usual from the outside world, and hardly appeared to be aware of the visitor's presence.

'My mother is very deaf,' Reynard explained, 'but don't try and shout – she can understand lip movements best.'

He went to the sideboard, and brought out a bottle of sherry (kept for ceremonial occasions) and three glasses. He found that his hands were trembling as he poured out the wine. The odd sense of exaltation which the apparition of Roy Archer had produced in him persisted; he was aware, moreover, though he told himself that it was absurd, of some lurking element of danger in their encounter – a danger indefinable yet strangely disturbing.

'I say, this is jolly nice of you,' the visitor exclaimed, as Reynard handed him the sherry. 'It's a rotten night outside – I nearly got blown into the ditch, up on the downs. D'you know that bit of road up by the Roman Camp?'

Reynard nodded.

'Well, you get the full force of the gale there – the old bus nearly tipped over. I ought to have known better than to come that way – it's a bit of road I know pretty well, too.'

'The camp isn't Roman, really,' Reynard said, for the sake of conversation.

'No, I know it's not. They call it that, though. It's probably Danish or Saxon.'

'British,' Reynard countered.

The other man's eyes met his.

'Interested in that sort of thing?'

'Yes, I've done a bit in that line,' Reynard admitted.

Archer turned back to his hostess and, as he spoke to her, Reynard studied him with a close interest. Tall, athletically built, he was obviously immensely strong, though his gentle movements and restrained manner seemed designed to disguise the fact. This dormant strength of body was reflected in the set of his features: his long-boned, rather predatory face wore habitually an expression of rather incongruous gentleness. His lips, beneath a small blond moustache, were parted even now in a smile of almost feminine amiability; yet one had the impression that those same lips would not, on other occasions, be wanting in firmness and decision. His hair, still gleaming with raindrops, was noticeable: of a light straw colour, and inclined to curl, it was cropped extremely short, and parted in the middle.

Presently Archer rose to go.

'We'll be seeing some more of each other,' he remarked quietly, with the air of one stating a self-evident and incontrovertible fact.

Once again Reynard felt the strange uprush of emotion which had overtaken him at the moment of Archer's arrival.

'I'm sorry you've got to go,' he said.

'Yes – fact is, I've promised to look in at a boxing tournament – some of our lads from the regiment are performing. Don't know if you're interested, but one of 'em – Spike Mandeville, our prize

heavyweight – he's a lovely fighter, really worth looking at . . .
Hullo!' he broke off, suddenly catching sight of the photograph of
Reynard's father. 'I say, don't think me frightfully rude, but was he
any relation of yours?'

'My father.'

'Good Lord, yes – why, I can remember him when I first joined
the regiment. Of course, he'd been retired for a long time, but he
was a pal of the present colonel, you know, and we used to see
something of him.'

He turned to Mrs Langrish and repeated to her, as well as he
could, what he had just been saying. Then, turning back to
Reynard, he grinned at him amiably.

'Of course,' he muttered, 'that's why the C.O. was so keen on
our – I mean, my. . . .' He broke off, and once again, puzzled,
Reynard perceived the tinge of embarrassment in his face, as
though his last words had been ill-judged. 'Well, well,' he said,
with a sudden assumption of heartiness, 'mustn't keep you standing around. If you wouldn't mind just showing me the way. . . .'

'I'll come a bit of the way with you, if you like,' Reynard offered,
'and put you on the right road.'

'No, no – I couldn't let you do that.'

'I'd like to,' Reynard insisted. 'I usually go out for a breath of air
about this time. The rain's stopped, too, by the sound of it.'

'Well, that's uncommonly decent of you. I suppose. . . .' he
paused, and fixed Reynard with his bright, rain-dark eyes, '. . . I
suppose you wouldn't care to run into the town and have a look at
the boxing?'

Reynard's heart leapt; a suddenly inexplicable happiness overcame him. His eyes met those of his new friend, and silently he gave
his assent.

'If you're sure your mother'll be all right,' Archer said
quietly.

Reynard, leaning over his mother's chair, explained rapidly that
he would be going out for an hour or two, and asked her not to wait
up. Mrs Langrish nodded placidly: she was not a nervous woman,
and was accustomed to being left alone.

The two men left the house. Outside the wind had dropped, and
a soft rain was falling. A dog barked in the valley, and from far
away, over towards Glamber, came the faint sound of a bugle.

Reynard listened to the sound with some surprise.

'I've never heard bugles from here before,' he remarked.

'Haven't you?' Archer queried, holding the car door open for him.

'You could hardly hear them all the way from Glamber.'

'How do you know that's coming from Glamber?'

'Well, there are no soldiers nearer than that, so far as I know.'

'I daresay you're right,' the other replied, with what seemed to Reynard a curiously off-hand air. 'Never mind, anyway. Jump in – we're late already.'

CHAPTER THREE

Not Marked on the Ordnance Map

The boxing tournament was held in the town's Territorial drill-hall. Reynard and his friend occupied ring-side seats: the boxing had already begun when they arrived, but the chief items of interest, Archer assured him, were yet to come.

For Reynard, the experience was something of a novelty: he had hardly ever attended a boxing match before, and knew very little about it. He found himself, however, before long entirely absorbed in the spectacle. Beneath the brilliant lights the naked figures advanced and retreated, grappling, feinting, lunging; now balanced in a statuesque immobility, now galvanized into a sudden frenzy of violence. The crowd cheered, the smoke-laden atmosphere grew thicker; the fighting, so it seemed to Reynard, became more violent with each successive bout. His own excitement grew with that of the crowd; had it occurred to him to think of it, he would hardly have recognized in himself the Reynard Langrish who, on this very same evening, only a few hours ago, had been torturing himself with fears of 'dissolution', or of the loss of what he believed to be his 'identity' . . .

In one of the brief intervals he turned to Archer with a sudden impulse of gratitude.

'It was awfully good of you to bring me,' he said.

'Only too pleased,' Archer replied, with an amiable grin.

Looking round the crowded hall, Reynard had a curious impression that the packed audience was united by some deep and unadmitted bond which he couldn't identify – something, it seemed, other than a mere interest in the boxing. He mentioned this impression to his companion, who looked at him sharply, and then smiled.

'You're learning things to-night, aren't you?' he chuckled. Then, since the next fight was about to begin, he turned back to the ring, leaving Reynard, not for the first time that evening, slightly puzzled.

Presently it was the turn of Spike Mandeville, the man from Archer's regiment. He was matched against a famous local heavyweight: the fight promised to be the star performance of the evening.

Spike Mandeville was a thick-set, heavily muscled man of about thirty, sandy-haired, red-faced, with a tooth or two missing. He looked a typical prizefighter of the old school. His opponent was taller, less heavily built, a dark-haired, dark-skinned man from one of the local collieries.

During the first round both men sparred cautiously: the miner seemed nervous. In the second round the soldier went in to the attack, landing a series of well-placed punches on the other's body. Spurred into action at last, the miner led off fiercely in the third round, and the soldier's smooth white skin was soon patched with angry red. His face an expressionless mask, Spike was biding his time.

'You wait,' muttered Archer between rounds. 'You wait till he springs that left hook of his. . . . There you are, I told you so! Oh, good man! Look at that! He's down! He's had it!'

The crowd roared; flail-like, the referee's hand marked the count – five, six, seven. . . . The miner was up again, his face bleeding, his dark matted hair dangling over his eyes. Attacking with a fierce desperation, he bludgeoned his way through the soldier's defence, and brought home a punch or two at Spike's head. It was evident, however, that the miner was finished – or very nearly so. Spike seemed to be playing with him, cat-like: the comedy continued almost till the end of the round, when suddenly, as though tiring of his game, the soldier planted a straight left at the miner's chin. A howl rose from the crowd; once again the miner lay prone, his chest heaving, his dark hair tumbled over his bruised, bleeding face. The flail-like beats knelled his defeat: Spike, his arm raised, faced the crowd. Watching him, Reynard noticed, with an odd sense that the detail was in some way significant, the design tattooed on his forearm: a red and blue snake curled about a naked sword.

After the boxing Archer suggested a drink at a pub nearby.

Unusually elated by the evening's entertainment, Reynard soon found the beer going to his head. He had become unaccustomed to alcohol of late, and perhaps the nervous tension of the last weeks had made him more liable to feel its effects. At all events, he found himself talking to his new friend with a fluency which surprised himself. He had already thanked Roy – whom he now called by his Christian name – half a dozen times for his kindness in bringing him; he now proceeded to do so all over again.

'Glad you enjoyed it,' Roy replied, as equably as ever. 'You must come along some other night. . . . I suppose,' he said, changing his tone, 'I suppose you saw some service – in the war, I mean?'

Reynard nodded.

'Army?'

'Oh, yes, the Army. I was in the —shires. I – I didn't have a commission, you know. I was in the ranks.'

Roy nodded.

'Yes, I know,' he muttered. 'I mean –' he grinned pleasantly, '– well, you know what I mean. Better off as an other rank, really.'

Puzzled once again by Roy's manner, and made bold by the beer he had drunk, Reynard decided to risk a direct question.

'I wish you'd tell me,' he said, 'what you meant earlier on to-night – just as we were leaving the house.'

'Yes? What did I say?' Roy's smile was almost fatuous in its complacency. 'Nothing rude, I hope?'

'No, it was something you said – about the C.O. – about you and I being —'

'Yes? It sounds fairly harmless, anyway. But what exactly *did* I say? I can't remember, for the life of me.'

'Something about the C.O. saying that you and I . . .' Reynard stopped, perplexedly; Roy's odd remark had haunted his mind the whole evening; he had tried already, on several occasions, to summon the courage to ask what he had meant by it; and now that the moment had come, his memory failed him entirely. Rack his brains as he might, Roy's puzzling words escaped him. Perhaps, after all, he had never really uttered them; probably he had said something quite ordinary, and he, Reynard, had entirely misunderstood him. . . .

Aware that Roy must think his behaviour foolish, he shook his head and gave a sudden laugh.

'I'm damned if *I* can remember now,' he said.

Roy chuckled.

'It couldn't have been anything very important, in that case,' he said. Smiling still, he was regarding Reynard, none the less, with a singular intentness. Presently his gaze shifted, and Reynard, following the direction of his eyes, saw that they were fixed upon a man who had just walked up to the counter. The man was in shirt sleeves, and his arms were elaborately tattooed.

'Ever had it done?' Roy asked suddenly, in a low voice.

Reynard started.

'Ever had *what* done?' he queried.

Roy nodded towards the man at the counter.

'Tattooing – like that bloke there,' he explained.

'Good heavens, no. Why ever should I?' Even as he spoke, Reynard remembered with a singular clarity the design on the arm of Spike Mandeville, the boxer, which he had noticed at the end of the fight: a snake wreathed about a sword.

'Oh, I dunno – lots of blokes have it done.' Roy paused for a moment, then said casually: 'Ever think of signing on again?'

'In the Army? No, I certainly haven't thought of it.' Reynard was aware that his voice sounded exaggeratedly loud: the beer had undoubtedly gone to his head – he would have to be careful.

'You might do worse, you know,' Roy suggested.

'But I was invalided out last time,' Reynard explained. 'I had rheumatic fever.'

'Yes, I know . . . I mean I understand that; I see your point – but you're quite fit again now, aren't you?'

'Oh, well, I suppose so – yes, I'm pretty fit on the whole.'

Roy ordered another couple of pints.

'I'll be tight,' Reynard exclaimed, speaking, as he was uncomfortably aware, a little too loudly.

'Won't hurt you once in a while,' Roy paid for the beer, and handed his mug to Reynard. 'But we'll have to get you fit again, you know, if you're coming back to us,' he said, his voice suddenly serious.

Reynard stared at him in astonishment. 'But I'm not coming back!' he exclaimed, stung to a sudden irritation, and speaking almost angrily.

Roy laughed.

'All right, old boy – don't lose your wool. I only meant – oh, well, *you* know,' and the bony, predatory face was once again wreathed in amiable smiles.

'But I *don't* know – I've not the least idea what you're getting at,' Reynard retorted. Baffled and irritated by Roy's behaviour, he wondered vaguely what could be the cause of it: was the man merely being incoherent and silly, or had his words any hidden meaning?

'What I mean is –' Roy was still fumbling over his words – 'it only struck me that you were probably rather keen on the Service, and – well, the point is —'

'But I don't. . . .' Reynard began again, and broke off as a young man entered the bar and loudly accosted Roy. The newcomer and Reynard were rapidly introduced – too rapidly for Reynard to catch the name, but he inferred, rightly as it happened, that the young man was a subaltern in Roy's regiment. He, too, had attended the boxing tournament, and the conversation for the next few minutes became entirely technical. Reynard, in whom the beer had induced a mood of placid tolerance, listened in silence. The young officer was a short, thick-set man, with firm, rather severe features and a small black moustache. Reynard noticed that his dark hair was parted, like Roy Archer's, in the middle: a curious coincidence nowadays, when such a coiffure was rather unfashionable. Presently the two men's talk switched to Army 'shop': Reynard, eavesdropping without much interest, caught references to some training operation, and noticed that Roy (for the second time that evening) mentioned 'The Dog' at Clambercrown, a long disused public house in the remote country beyond Priorsholt. Some detachment, it appeared, was stationed there for a period of intensive training. . . . The curious name stirred in Reynard a vague childhood memory: he remembered how, on a number of occasions, he had tried to find the place, wandering for whole days at a time over the lonely, wooded hills, but without success. The inn called 'The Dog' had been long untenanted, even at that date; and the name, Clambercrown, seemed to be the vaguest of indications, referring to nothing so definite as a village or hamlet, but merely to an ill-defined woodland district, never delimited,· not marked on the ordnance map. It was odd, Reynard thought, that 'The Dog at Clambercrown' should have survived as a landmark for Army manoeuvres.

In the close, smoke-filled atmosphere, Reynard began to feel unmistakably drunk; he became aware that the two officers were addressing him, but he had lost the thread of the conversation, and found himself answering yes or no with an air of assumed intelligence which, it seemed to him, could hardly have deceived anybody.

Roy and his friend, however, seemed perfectly satisfied with his replies.

'That's fine, then,' exclaimed the dark young officer. 'We'll be meeting again before long in that case.'

Supposing that he must have accepted some kind of invitation without realizing its nature, Reynard blushed scarlet and, to cover his confusion, escaped to the urinal. When he returned, the dark young man had gone; and shortly afterwards Roy suggested that it was time to start for home. By this time the beer had made Reynard sleepy, and during the drive home he fell into a half-doze. He was not conscious at the time of having done so; but it was only thus that he was able, the next day, to account for a curious memory which haunted him – a remark of Roy's uttered at the very moment when the car pulled up at the gate of his mother's house: 'We'll have to see about starting your training.' He must, he supposed, have fallen asleep just before the car stopped, and the nonsensical words had been part of some brief, truncated dream

'I'll be seeing you soon,' Roy said in farewell. His tone implied more than a mere social formula: quite evidently he meant what he said. 'I'll be coming into the bank – to-morrow, probably,' he added, as the car moved off.

Reynard listened to the diminishing roar of the engine as his friend drove off up the hill and away towards Glamber. In the silence which followed the last faint vibration, he suddenly detected another sound: the remote throb of an aeroplane engine, far away to the south-east where, beyond the wooded hills, lay the mysterious territory called Clambercrown.

CHAPTER FOUR

Like Blown Leaves

The next morning Reynard woke with a sense of well-being such as he had not experienced for a considerable time. The sensation was hard to account for: a chance acquaintance had taken him to a boxing tournament – hardly an event calculated to change the course of his life; yet if he had fallen in love or inherited a fortune, the difference in his mood could scarcely have been more marked.

The morning was fine after the night's rain; the bus ride into Glamber over the high plateau of the downs was, for once, a pleasure consciously enjoyed. At the bank he worked assiduously and with an unusual efficiency. Naturally poor at figures, he was aware that the work cost him, on a normal day, far more effort than it did most of his colleagues; he had none of that mental slickness which is the chief virtue of the clerk, and he was compelled to check and re-check each transaction with a laboured slowness which often brought him into contempt. This morning, however, he felt, as the saying goes, 'on top of his work'. He felt, also, better disposed than usual towards his co-workers, with whom, generally speaking, he was on rather indifferent terms, since he shared few of their outside interests, and despised the complex snobberies which characterized their relations with each other. One man in particular Reynard had learnt to dislike – a pretentious youth named Garnett, who had obtained a commission in the Air Force during the war, and was apt to ape (or rather to parody, unconsciously) the manners of a 'gentleman'. To-day, however, even young Garnett seemed a tolerable companion, and Reynard surprised him (as well as himself) by suggesting that they took their lunch together at the Shamrock Tea-rooms, a cheap eating-place much patronized by the staff of the bank.

During the afternoon Reynard found himself watching, with an increasing impatience, for the appearance of Roy Archer. He had felt absolutely certain that his new friend would visit the bank to-day, though in fact Roy had made no definite promise. Until ten minutes to three he continued to watch; and only when the bank's doors were finally closed did he force himself, reluctantly, to accept the fact that Roy would not be coming after all. It was a bitter disappointment: yet he would have found it hard to explain why it meant so much to him. That a casual acquaintance could have assumed, overnight, so great an importance in his life, seemed ridiculous; yet such was the fact. The trip to Larchester was invested already, in Reynard's mind, with a romantic nostalgia – though he could remember, for that matter, very little about it. During the latter part of the evening he had certainly been rather drunk – a circumstance which he had confessed, not without certain rakish pride, to Ted Garnett. The beer, an unaccustomed indulgence, had perhaps accounted for the halo of romance which he had bestowed upon Roy Archer; and no doubt, too, it was the beer which was responsible for a certain perplexity which still haunted his mind. Several small details refused to be fitted logically into the remembered pattern of the evening: there was, for example, some curious remark about his colonel which Roy had made and never satisfactorily explained – indeed, there were several such remarks; there was also the episode of the mysterious bugle-call – nothing of importance, certainly, but (since there were no barracks within sound of Priorsholt) perplexing, and to Reynard, who was apt to worry himself unduly about such trifles, faintly disquieting.

Even after the bank closed, Reynard found himself glancing once or twice, hopefully, out of the windows, in case Roy should make a belated appearance. Owing to the care with which he had to-day dealt with his own work, and to the fact that business had been slacker than usual, he was able to leave the bank at a comparatively early hour. Riding homewards in the later afternoon, he was filled with an unaccustomed desire for some kind of activity; and reaching home an hour or so before the time for the evening meal he wandered out into the garden. Here he found that, on the waste patch commonly used for bonfires, a large pile of autumnal rubbish had collected: rose-prunings, dead stuff from the borders, discarded vegetables and paper cartons. On a sudden impulse, he went into the tool shed and collected a fork and spade, some old newspapers and a tin of paraffin. Then, returning to the rubbish-pile, he dug out two shallow trenches in the form of a cross, arranged loose screws of paper in the centre, and piled the drier rubbish – cartons and rose-clippings – loosely above it. He sprinkled the pile with paraffin, and flung a lighted match into its midst. A flame shot up: the dry stuff kindled with a satisfying crackle; then, as the fire burnt through, Reynard added the damper fuel slowly, till a column of dense white smoke ascended in the still air.

The evening, windless and mild, faded gently into dusk; in the darkening air, the recurrent spurts of flame shot up with an increasing brilliance. In the meadow beyond the garden, a herd of cattle, bound for the neighbouring farm, passed lowing beneath the bronze canopy of an enormous chestnut; overhead, rooks wheeled like blown leaves, intensely black against the last pale light. Punctually feeding the fire, waiting with an almost greedy anticipation for the next spurt of flame, Reynard felt a peculiar happiness blossom in his mind. It was many weeks since he had made a bonfire, or attended to any of the other simple domestic tasks which he had once been in the habit of performing. To-night, more than on any other occasion which he could remember, the bonfire seemed to offer a singular fulfilment: it was as though he were performing some kind of private ritual, an act necessary to his mode of life, which had been too long neglected or forgotten.

As the fire blazed higher, its heat, combined with the mildness of the air, made him sweat: he took off his coat, then his tie, and unbuttoned his shirt. The touch of his own warm, naked flesh seemed curiously alien to him: a reminder of the life of the body which, in recent months, had played almost no part in his existence. Moving to and fro about the fire, forking the rubbish into position, he felt a renewed sense of purely physical well-being; and it was with regret (though he was ready enough for his food) that he heard his mother's voice calling him in to tea.

He washed quickly in cold water, and, sitting down at the table, began to eat with a relish which was unusual for him nowadays. His mother noticed this with pleasure, and pressed more food upon him. His sense of well-being increased; after the meal, he lit a cigarette, half hoping that he would be able, once again, to enjoy its flavour. The cigarette, however, was as tasteless as ever, and he felt a momentary disappointment. The ability to taste tobacco had become for him lately a kind of test of his state of health; when the flavour returned it would mean that he had recovered, finally, from his indisposition.

His cigarette failed to satisfy him; but he felt, to-night, more confident than of late that his 'recovery' was not far off. His mood of confidence, moreover, helped to minimize another disappointment – the non-appearance of Roy Archer at the bank. After all, Roy had not definitely promised to come; no doubt he would call in to-morrow or the next day.

After tea Reynard returned to the bonfire, and for some time continued to stoke it, till at last the whole of the pile was consumed. He lingered in the garden, watching the fire's dying glow, and listening to the faint night noises: a dog's bark, the distant whistle of a train, the rumble of the Glamber bus from the main road. Suddenly, in an interlude of unbroken silence, he caught another and different sound; it came, not as he would have expected, from the direction of Glamber, but from the opposite quarter – inexplicable, charged with mystery: the faint, far calling of a bugle, sounding the 'Last Post'.

CHAPTER FIVE

Between Sea and Sky

The next day went by, and the next, and still Roy Archer made no appearance at the bank. Perhaps, after all, thought Reynard, his promise had been a mere piece of conventional politeness; yet he could not honestly believe this; and since Roy, in any case, had an account at the bank, he would be certain to come in sooner or later.

At last, four days after his visit to Priorsholt, he appeared: strolling into the bank ten minutes before closing-time, when Reynard had given up expecting him. He showed no sign whatever of recognizing Reynard, and walked straight over to another compartment, at the counter, where he was served by Ted Garnett, with whom he remained in conversation till after the doors were closed. Reynard waited, mastering his impatience, till he should have finished his talk with Garnett; fully expecting that he would then pause on his way out to pass the time of day, and perhaps to arrange a rendezvous for the evening. But to Reynard's astonishment, Roy walked straight out of the bank without so much as turning his head.

Reynard's first impulse was to follow his friend precipitately out of the bank and demand an explanation; his second, to hurry round to Ted Garnett and ask him if Roy had left any message. As it was, he did neither of these things; a customer happening to approach him at that moment, he was forced to concentrate for several minutes upon business; and by the time the customer – an exacting middle-class woman – had taken her departure, he found that his first indignation had subsided. There must, he felt sure, be some explanation of his friend's odd behaviour; nor could he bring himself to believe (though the humiliating thought did occur to him) that Roy had 'cut' him for merely snobbish reasons. Had Roy been of a different class, it was conceivable that he might have considered Ted Garnett (on account of his war-time commission) more eligible for public recognition than himself; but Roy most certainly was incapable of any such petty bourgeois prejudice. No doubt, Reynard thought, they would meet again shortly, and his friend's apparent defection would be satisfactorily explained. . . . Meanwhile, he hurried through the rest of his work, anxious to get home as early as possible, for he had planned to dig over one of the herbaceous borders in the garden.

An hour later, walking down the High Street towards the Town Hall, where he was in the habit of catching his bus, he had almost forgotten Roy's visit. He was the more surprised, therefore, when a familiar voice hailed him from a car parked by the pavement.

'There you are at last – I was waiting for you,' Roy exclaimed. 'Jump in, we'll go and have some tea.'

'I – I ought to go home, really,' Reynard stammered, his surprise making him incoherent.

'Never mind, I'll drive you home later. Jump in and don't argue,' Roy ordered, with good-natured violence.

Reynard obeyed without further protest, half-aware, with a vague sense of humiliation, that his prompt compliance was a relic of his own training as a soldier. As Roy drove off he was about to ask the reason for his friend's odd behaviour of the afternoon, but a sudden delicacy restrained him; if Roy, he decided, had had a reason (as no doubt he had) for ignoring him, it was very probably one which he would not care to discuss.

Roy drove on without speaking, through the narrow streets behind the Town Hall, and up the steep hill towards the cliff tops.

'Where are we going?' Reynard asked.

'I thought we'd have tea at the "Valiant Trooper",' Roy explained. 'We can have a drink there later and then I'll drive you home. I've got plenty of petrol,' he added, with a grin. 'They seem to think my job's important enough to justify it.'

The 'Valiant Trooper' was a small public house situated in an isolated position on the cliff tops. Beyond it the high chalklands swept away inland towards Priorsholt and Larchester; below the town of Glamber lay tumbled across a funnel-shaped valley, smudged with smoke and sea mist. Across the valley, on the other side of the town, the grim grey barracks impended heavily above the narrow streets; at intervals a bugle call trembled faintly on the still evening air.

In the small inn parlour a slatternly woman served them with tea; an enormous purple birthmark disfigured her face, and she took their orders silently, as though somewhat resentful of their presence. Reynard sensed her hostility, and, when she had left them, mentioned it to Roy.

'Oh, it's not a bad little place,' Roy observed, 'and old Mother Tantrip's all right, really. I use it quite a lot, it's convenient for –' He broke off, grinned, and said: 'Have some more toast.'

The daylight faded as they took their tea; afterwards they strolled out into the garden at the back to wait, as Roy said, for the bar to open. The garden extended to the verge of the cliff; only an insecure fence separated it from the abyss. The whole place seemed to Reynard to have an air of instability – a small world poised precariously between sea and sky, possessing no firm roots in the solid earth. Few visitors used the inn for tea at this season, and the garden had a squalid, derelict appearance; a few fading asters wilted in the borders, and a clump of Michaelmas daisies sprawled against the boundary-fence, their subdued fires smouldering dully in the dying light.

'Good weather,' Roy remarked, sniffing appreciatively the mild air. The sky was cloudless, the sea lay smooth as a plate below the cliffs, tinged with the faint colours of the sunset; gulls wheeled fitfully below the garden, their shrill cries softened by the far murmur of the waves. Roy stood silently for several minutes, staring out to sea; suddenly he turned to Reynard.

'Thought any more about your training?' he asked.

Roy's face appeared shadowy and insubstantial in the dim light; even his voice seemed, in this desolate eyrie above the sea, to have a vague, disembodied quality. Reynard had a curious impression that the surprising words had been not so much spoken as projected by some telepathic means into his own consciousness. He remained silent, and when Roy, a moment or two later, repeated his question, he started, taken by surprise.

'What did you say?' he queried, unsteadily.

'This training of yours. We were talking about it, you know, in the "Royal Oak" that night.'

'But *what* training? I don't know. I don't remember.'

Roy chuckled.

'Of course you do – don't be so vague. I'd have contacted you before, but we're going in for this scheme in a big way, and I don't get much time to see personal friends. It's going pretty well, too, I don't mind saying – we're getting so many re-enlistments, local ones, that we hardly know what to do with 'em. The militia huts are crowded out, and we had to put the last intake under canvas. It's pretty rough, but the lads don't mind – they're most of them used to active service conditions, and of course the pay's pretty good. By the time you come up we ought to have things straightened out a bit more.'

The whole of this speech was delivered in Roy's habitual matter-of-fact tones; but as it proceeded Reynard could detect a note of mounting enthusiasm. Bewildered, he made no reply, and after a pause Roy continued, speaking now more directly, more confidentially, than before:

'One thing worth remembering – if you're thinking of putting in for a commission this time, you ought to do something about it right away. At the moment it's pretty easy; but you know what it is – the longer things go on, the more sticky the authorities get. I'm always thankful I got through my O.C.T.U. when I did – the blokes that came up afterwards had a hell of a time.'

'But I don't see –' Reynard interjected at last, 'I don't really see why –' he broke off, his bewilderment so mastering him that he could find no words to express it. It was evident that, at their previous meeting, Roy and his friend must have persuaded him – or entrapped him – into some promise or agreement which he couldn't now remember; probably the beer had been responsible. He did, very vaguely, remember some talk of 'training'; but what sort of training, or in what connection, he couldn't recall. No doubt, he decided, it was something to do with the Territorials.

Meanwhile Roy had begun to speak again with an easy casualness which, to Reynard's bewildered mind, seemed to imply a whole set of unspoken premises with which he, Reynard, was assumed to be conversant. Roy was now describing, in some detail, the training scheme itself: it included running (long distance and sprinting), unarmed combat ('you remember that from the war'), a graduated course of P.T., squad-drill and swimming; wrestling and boxing also played a part. ('You'll like the boxing – I might even get Spike Mandeville to coach you a bit.') Listening to his friend's easy, matter-of-fact exposition of the scheme, Reynard found his initial bewilderment giving place to a kind of hypnotic conviction that he had, after all, grasped (or almost grasped) what Roy was 'getting at'. There had been occasions during his schooldays (which he still sometimes remembered with shame) when, after some algebraic equation had been repeatedly expounded to him, he would persuade himself, with a mental dishonesty born of fear, that he had understood it at last, though in fact the problem remained as obscure to him as ever. Now, once again, as he listened to Roy's explanations of his 'scheme', he found that, by the mere force of his desire to understand, he was actually beginning (or so it seemed) to do so. The immediate necessity for 'training', the idea of enlisting in some form of 'Territorial' organisation, seemed no longer a rather frightening mystery, but a quite reasonable and intelligible plan. Indeed, once he had conquered his initial distrust, he began to find the prospect curiously attractive. During the last few days, his renewed enthusiasm for gardening had improved his state of health to a surprising extent; perhaps a spell of hard physical exercise was what he needed; at all events, as he listened to his friend's voice in the gathering dusk, he felt a growing eagerness to know when exactly the 'programme' was due to start, and on what date he would be expected to present himself for instruction.

Presently, as Roy paused in his discourse, Reynard questioned him as to details.

'Oh, I'll take you out myself for the first few weeks,' Roy promised. 'We'll just get you limbered up a bit – running, a bit of sparring, and so on. We can start to-morrow, if you like – I'm usually free about this time. I can pick you up by the Town Hall, like I did to-day, and we can put in an hour or two before you go home.'

The darkness was now almost complete: the sea was hardly visible, but the town below the cliffs was brightly lit. Far out across the bay the lighthouse winked from its remote headland; in the clear violet sky a star or two came out, and a crescent moon rode high above the darkened channel.

'Time we went and saw old Mother Tantrip and got a drink,' Roy suggested.

They went into the bar, now brightly lit, and Roy ordered two pints of bitter. A few other men were present – mostly young and athletic-looking, perhaps soldiers in civilian clothes; Roy appeared to know them, for he nodded familiarly to them across the bar.

'You won't regret it, I can tell you,' Roy said. 'The training, I mean. I feel a hell of a lot fitter myself since I started. Of course, nobody knows how long the emergency's going to last, but in any case, it's all in a good cause.'

Several times during the course of his friend's talk Reynard had noticed the recurrence of this word 'emergency'; at first it had puzzled him, but he no longer felt disposed to enquire too closely into the terms which Roy employed. By 'emergency', he supposed, Roy meant merely the general situation as it had existed since the war; indeed, an 'emergency' did still officially exist – it had never been rescinded. He felt a passing sense of guilt at his own ignorance of international affairs: remembering his scamped perusal of *The Times*, the headlines which, even as he looked at them, seemed to merge into an unmeaning blur. The 'Crisis', so it seemed to him, had become a kind of permanent mental climate: one accepted it, as one accepted the weather, or the bank's working hours, without questioning it, or expecting it to be otherwise.

Over a second pint Roy became still more confidential. He spoke in lowered tones, almost conspiratorially; there was a curious glint of excitement in his eyes.

'Between you and me,' he murmured, 'it rather looks as if things are blowing up faster than most people think. I've been in contact with one or two high-ups recently, and though of course they don't *say* anything, one can't help reading between the lines.'

Reynard, whom the beer had made, as usual, more receptive and less critical, listened with an increasing interest. If he didn't, even now, understand all that Roy's talk implied, he had, as he believed, a fairly good idea of the ground-work. On the very first evening, when his friend had come to Priorsholt, Reynard had felt a curious conviction of Roy's authority; at the time, of course, he had been ignorant as to the nature of this authority; but even then, at that first meeting, his heart had made, as it were, an inward gesture of assent, a pledge of loyalty which required no formal oath to substantiate it.

'And I've a shrewd idea,' Roy was saying, 'that the other side's getting dug in – not openly, of course: officially it's only a routine affair – but one can't help seeing and hearing things, and it looks as if they're concentrating a lot of staff up by Bladbean and Clamber-crown. Of course, it may just be bluff, but some of our blokes seem pretty certain they're up to no good. . . .'

Muzzy after his second pint, Reynard took little note of Roy's words; he was content to watch the healthy, weathered face close to his own, the eyes which seemed like dark pools, the mobile lips beneath the short, bristly moustache. Presently it was time to go. They walked out of the bar to where Roy had parked his car; the night was very still, little traffic passed on the main road, and the crying of the gulls was silenced. Roy got into the car without a word, and Reynard followed him. It seemed to Reynard that he must have misjudged the position of the inn, for in an extraordinarily short time the car pulled up before his mother's house.

Pressed to come in for a drink, Roy refused, politely but firmly.

'Too much to do,' he grinned. 'Don't forget, then – to-morrow night, same time, same place. Better bring a pair of shorts – and have you got any running shoes? Good-oh – I'll be seeing you, then. Cheerio!'

He started up the car and drove off. Entering the house, Reynard was aware that he must be far later than usual, and mentioned the fact, apologetically, to his mother. Mrs Langrish, however, accepted his lateness with her usual placidity; and indeed, when he came to look at the clock, he found that it was, in fact, not nearly so late as he had imagined. He must, he supposed, have left the bank earlier than he had thought.

Later that evening he walked out into the garden for a short airing before going to bed. Once again, in the stillness, he fancied that he could catch the far cry of a bugle; and found himself recalling something Roy had said about 'Bladbean and Clambercrown'. He had not taken much notice of the remark at the time; now, however, an idea recurred to him which had haunted his mind for some days past. The mysterious region known as Clambercrown lay over beyond the hills towards the south-east; and it was from this very quarter that the bugle calls appeared to come. He tried vainly to remember what exactly it was that Roy had said about that particular district; but he was tired, he had drunk two pints of beer, and Roy's words, whatever they had been, eluded him completely. Yet, as he stood there straining his ears in the darkness, another older memory recurred to him: he remembered, once again, those days in his early boyhood when he had wandered for miles over the wooded hills, searching for the abandoned inn called the 'Dog'. He had never found it: but one hot August afternoon, trekking through the stifling thickets, he had emerged suddenly into a clearing to find himself surrounded by soldiers. They were, he had afterwards heard, a battalion of infantry, encamped in that lonely spot for certain special field exercises . . . terrified by their red, grinning faces, he had turned and fled along the path by which he had come, pursued by laughter and catcalls. The incident had so impressed him that for years he had not dared to resume his search for the 'Dog' at Clambercrown; and by the time he had grown out of his irrational fear, he found that his long-cherished desire to find the inn had vanished also.

CHAPTER SIX

A Dual Image

Reynard awoke the next morning filled with a peculiar, compulsive excitement, the cause of which he could not, for some minutes, analyse. Suddenly he remembered: it was to-day that he was to begin his 'training'.

His excitement was half-pleasurable, half-fearful; and he was aware of a certain relief that, in spite of his promise to undergo a course of what Roy sometimes called 'rehabilitation', he had not, as yet, committed himself to any definite form of enlistment. For some reason or other he found the whole affair impossible to explain to his mother, and, before his departure for the bank, was careful to tell her that he should probably be kept late at his work, and not to wait supper for him. There was no particular reason why he should have invented this tale; nor, indeed, need he have troubled to explain that the dispatch-case which he carried contained some papers which he had been working on at home – its actual contents being a pair of football shorts and the canvas running shoes which he had retained from his Army kit. There was nothing surely in the least reprehensible about Roy's 'training-programme'; yet it seemed to him essential that his mother should not know of it; apart from anything else, it would probably 'worry' her, possibly she might fancy that there was some danger of an imminent war. . . .

As it happened his instinct for secrecy seemed to be justified when, during the morning, Roy came into the bank. On this occasion Ted Garnett was already occupied with a customer, and Roy made straight for Reynard's compartment. They exchanged polite greetings; Roy proffered a cheque for ten pounds and, while Reynard cashed it, commented upon the weather (which remained warm and cloudless), the day's news and a film at the local cinema. He seemed in rather a hurry, and as soon as he had counted his money began to move away. Reynard, remembering that they had fixed no definite time for their evening rendezvous, plucked up his courage and spoke – rather loudly, for Roy had already turned away from the counter.

'I say,' he called after the retreating figure, 'I forgot to tell you – I might be a bit late to-night.'

Roy wheeled round, turning upon Reynard a countenance in which his habitual amiability was mingled with a rather fatuous incomprehension.

'Sorry – were you speaking to me?' he queried. 'I didn't quite catch. . . ?'

Knowing that he had spoken with perfect distinctness and fearful, moreover, of attracting the other clerks' attention, Reynard dropped his eyes apologetically.

'No, I'm sorry,' he murmured, 'I was speaking to someone else.'

'Oh, sorry, laddie – I thought you were talking to me.' He grinned pleasantly and walked, with his jaunty, athletic stride, out of the bank.

Of course, Reynard reflected, one might have known that Roy wouldn't want to talk about the 'training-scheme' in the bank. He had been foolish to mention to-night's meeting; no doubt his friend would be there at the usual time, and would wait for him. In future, he would have to pretend that Roy was merely an ordinary customer, whom he had never met (or was likely to meet) outside. Evidently Roy had expected him to take this course without being told; and the thought of his indiscretion troubled him for the rest of the day with a disproportionate sense of guilt.

It was, as it happened, somewhat later than usual when Reynard left the bank that afternoon. He had walked down to the Town Hall, half-fearing (and half-hoping, for he was nervous of the ordeal before him) that Roy would not have waited. Roy's car, however, was in its usual place, and Roy's pleasant, rather vapid smile greeted him.

'In you get,' Roy exclaimed, 'We've no time to waste.'

'I'm sorry I'm so late,' Reynard apologised. 'I meant to tell you I might be . . . Have you been waiting long?'

Roy shook his head.

'I've only just got here myself,' he said.

Reynard climbed into the car, and Roy drove off in the same

direction as before, up the steep hill towards the cliff-tops and the 'Valiant Trooper'. This puzzled Reynard, who had expected to be taken to the barracks at the western end of the town; he kept discreetly silent, however, fearing that Roy might resent being questioned unnecessarily.

Roy drove on in silence past the 'Valiant Trooper', then turned inland along a narrow, chalky road leading uphill over a high sweep of downland. The road narrowed, became a track, and petered out at last by a group of disused Nissen huts. Instead of stopping the car Roy drove on recklessly across the uneven turf, the car bumping and swaying violently; the ground began to rise more steeply, then levelled into a broad, sweeping plateau. Reynard suddenly recognized the place.

'Why, it's the Roman Camp,' he exclaimed.

Roy half-turned to him in surprise.

'Of course,' he said. 'What did you think it was?'

He pulled up the car with a jolt at the border of the 'camp'. This consisted of a vaguely defined system of earthworks ranged about a flattened central platform.

'Of course, it's no more Roman than I am,' Roy remarked.

'Nobody knows much about it, anyway,' said Reynard, who had at one time made a study of local archaeological findings. 'They did a bit of digging about thirty years ago, but nothing much turned up. There were a few bronze implements, and a sort of amulet-thing – they've got it in the Glamber museum.'

Roy nodded.

'I know, I've seen it – a snake and a dagger. Supposed to be "Druidic", but that's all balls, probably. No one knows anything about the Druids, anyway . . . . It's a lot of cock, really, half the stuff they tell you.'

Reynard had an odd impression that Roy was assuming a consciously 'low-brow' pose, and that his interest in the subject was wider than he chose to admit.

'I should think the Camp is certainly pre-Roman, anyway,' Reynard sententiously remarked, half aware that his words were an attempt to gain time, to postpone the ordeal before him.

Roy, perhaps, detected this, for he made a sudden impatient movement.

'Time we got cracking,' he said. 'Jump out. Got your running-kit? Good – we might as well get stripped down. It's not cold.'

In the lee of the car Roy undressed himself rapidly and pulled on a pair of khaki shorts. Reynard, less briskly, followed his example; the evening was mild enough, but, unaccustomed as he was of late to such exposure, he felt the autumnal chill invading his body. At his side Roy was already marking time with raised knees, and thrashing his arms across his chest. His big body, though heavily built and muscular, was smooth and white as a child's; Reynard noted with surprise that his left forearm was tattooed – an unusual practice among the officer-caste. In the gathering dusk the mark was indistinct, and Reynard was unable to see what it represented; a vague memory stirred in his mind of some recent encounter – he couldn't recall when or with whom – at which he had observed a similar mark, and in precisely the same position on the left forearm.

'Ready?' barked Roy impatiently. 'Come on then – we'll just have a trot round the course to loosen you up.'

He set off, running at a steady pace with long, easy strides; Reynard, catching up with him, fell into step, breathing rather fast from the unaccustomed exertion, and shivering slightly as the full force of the breeze struck his bare flesh. Their course followed the boundaries of the chalk-plateau, an area of about twenty-five acres, confined within a broken-down wire fence. Beyond the fence, the land sloped away into more level fields, mostly arable, with here and there a small copse or a clump of beeches. Overhead, the clear sky seemed enormous, an airy void beneath which the land appeared a mere shrunken island poised between chasms of emptiness. The distances were lost in gathering dusk, familiar landmarks were obscured or distorted by the hallucinatory sunset light. High overhead a belated lark twittered vaguely and intermittently, as though insecurely moored to earth by its thin thread of sound. Unearthly too seemed the far cries of bugles from the distant barracks, invisible beyond the cliff-tops. Nothing in this high remote place seemed earthly or substantial: sound merged with sight, the blown grasses were an emanation of the wind itself, trees hung cloud-like above the horizon. Vaguely, without much surprise, Reynard realized that other runners, besides themselves, were circulating about the high dusky plateau. Their figures passed and repassed, silent and absorbed; some were perhaps soldiers from the barracks, others, possibly, as Reynard conjectured, merely volunteers like himself, undergoing their preliminary phase of training. No greetings were exchanged: plainly, it was no mere social occasion which had brought these athletes together in this out-of-the-way place, but a shared impulse, a sense of dedication to some high purpose. Dogged and silent, solitary or in pairs, they loped past in the gathering dusk: participants, it seemed, in some esoteric tribal rite, a community pledged to hardness and self-denial . . .

'. . . Most of 'em know it, too,' Roy was muttering in short breathless gasps. 'Of course, you can't – expect them – to grasp all the issues. They're not – educated blokes – most of 'em – though we do pick 'em pretty carefully. It's not the brainy ones – that make the best soldiers – all that stuff about education – you know, the citizen-soldier and all that business – it's all balls, really. Thank Christ they're beginning to realize it. . . . What we want's the honest-to-God, old-fashioned soldier – plenty of blood-lust – and none of your pansy nonsense about education. . . .'

It seemed to Reynard that they had been running for hours: breathless at first, and tortured by a 'stitch', he had at length found his second wind, and had settled down to the easy loping pace set by his companion. A brisk glow warmed his body, and his brain was unusually lucid, though the bounds of his consciousness seemed curiously extended. His sense of time appeared to be in some way modified: he could not tell, for instance, how long Roy had been talking – the short, breathless remarks seemed a kind of continuation of his own train of thought, but he could hardly have specified at exactly what point his reflections had merged into his friend's spoken words.

Nor could he have guessed how many times they had completed the course round the camp; once accustomed to the movement, he had ceased to notice the landmarks which, in any case, were now almost obliterated in the darkness. At last Roy called a halt, and they returned to the car. Huddled in their coats, they rested in silence for a few minutes; the first stars shone out, and from a neighbouring copse came the squawk of some night bird, sudden and disquieting.

'O.K.,' Roy remarked, after an interval, 'we'll have a few minutes' sparring, and then I should think we might call it a day. It'll have to be bare fists, I'm afraid – I haven't got a spare pair of mitts . . . O.K., then, I'll just give you an idea of the main outlines. . . . We'll have to get Spike to take you on later. . . . Right, now here's your first position – no, arms like this, see? No, watch me: you've got your feet wrong – the stance is important, you know. All right, then – here goes! No, you're letting me have it all my own

way – just concentrate on your defence, don't bother about trying
to hit back – you'll have plenty of chances to do that. . . .'

Awkward, nervous, fatigued from the running, Reynard obediently went through the motions under Roy's patient instruction.
The dimmed car lamps made a little world of brightness in the
surrounding dark, a world in which their two naked bodies were
the sole inhabitants. To Reynard, indeed, it seemed that beyond
the area of the light were stretched abysses of nothingness, of
non-existence: only this silent communion of conflict was real, a
dual image of reality now blurred in vagueness (as they sprang
apart) now concentrated to a focal point of clarity, as they fell into a
sudden clinch.

Roy, who in his capacity as instructor, had up till now delivered
no more than a gentle tap or two at his pupil's body, suddenly
planted a sharp stinging blow on the upper part of Reynard's chest,
following it up with a clip to the side of his head. A spasm of pure
physical anger spurred Reynard to a new alertness: his body was
suddenly intent and rigid, waiting with a fierce exultation for the
next blow. He countered it clumsily, and Roy's knuckles struck
him painfully above the right nipple. Another blow and another
stung his already tingling flesh: rage possessed him now, he wanted
passionately to hurt the big naked body of his instructor. He struck
out wildly, without science, blind with anger; his opponent, de-
fending himself with effortless ease, flicked the blows aside like so
many flies. For a moment, as Roy stepped into the full glare of the
light, Reynard saw his face: strong and predatory, like a wolf's, but
perfectly calm and inexpressive, the mouth curved in the habitual,
rather stupid smile. The sight stung Reynard to a new burst of
rage: he sprang in to the attack, and for a second caught Roy off his
guard. He hit out once again, mustering every ounce of his
strength, and with a savage joy saw his fist strike home full on
Roy's mouth. Roy gave a deep laugh and with a sudden movement,
seized Reynard's arms in a vice-like grip.

'You would, would you?' he chuckled.

Dull taut with anger, Reynard struggled for a moment, then,
aware of Roy's immensely superior strength, he allowed his
muscles to relax. His anger subsided; he felt, suddenly, an extreme
weakness steal over him. The sensation was curiously pleasant,
reminding him of the awakening from anaesthesia at the dentist's;
he would have liked to laugh aloud, to cry, to make some nonsensical remark. To his surprise, Roy continued to hold him prisoner:

raising his face to that of his friend, he observed the dark pool-like eyes and the full lips parted, as before, in a gentle inexpressive grin.

Reynard lowered his eyes, suddenly ashamed.

'I'm sorry,' he said, 'I lost my temper.'

Roy tightened his grip for a moment, and chuckled.

'That's just what I was waiting for,' he said.

'B – but why?' Reynard stammered.

'I wanted to be sure you'd hit back – I *wanted* you to lose your wool. Oh, I know it's not good boxing – you've got all the rules to learn still – but the point is, *you've got to learn to fight*, and you can't do that unless you've got some spunk in you. No amount of technique'll help you, if you can't get angry.'

The last words were spoken in a curiously exultant tone. Suddenly he relaxed his grip, and gave Reynard a parting tap on the shoulder. 'You're O.K., laddie – you'll do.'

He turned away and began to search for his clothes.

'Better hurry up and get dressed,' he remarked. 'We'll have one pint at the Trooper and then I'll run you home. . . . You'll have to ease up on the beer ration now you're in training. . . . Smoking, too – you ought to cut it out really. Does it worry you much?'

'I smoke a good deal,' Reynard admitted.

'I should try and give it up.' Roy spoke with what seemed to Reynard an excessive emphasis. 'It's not that there's any real physical harm in it – it's the psychological effect, you know.' Half-dressed, his shirt flapping over his trousers, he regarded Reynard with a singular intentness. 'It's a dirty habit, after all,' he added, pulling on his socks, 'and it's too easy to satisfy. . . . It's all very well for kids, but now you're one of us –' the words once more seemed over-emphasized – 'you ought to be able to do without it. I know it's difficult – I had a hell of a time when *I* gave it up – kept having lapses, you know, and felt bloody ashamed of myself. But it's worth it, in the long run.'

'I'll probably give it up,' Reynard replied. 'In any case, I can't taste a cigarette properly at the moment – I haven't been able to for some time. It's something to do with being "run-down", I suppose.'

Roy nodded.

'That's just it,' he said. 'You'll find it'll come back again – the taste, I mean. Give it up for a bit, and you'll find you'll enjoy it all the more when the time comes. Quite a good tip –' he added casually, 'at least, *I* found it useful – is never to smoke in bed, or when you're by yourself . . . Right – are you ready? Good, then we'll go and find that pint I promised you.'

He climbed into the car, and Reynard followed. The plateau was deserted now: the other 'trainees' (if such they had been) were gone. In the faint moonlight, a group of vague irregular shapes broke the level sweep of downland – the tumuli and earthworks comprising the so-called 'camp': desolate and untenanted once again, a house for the wind.

CHAPTER SEVEN

Eligible for Enlistment

Reynard's training proceeded fairly regularly during the next few weeks, according to the programme mapped out by Roy Archer. Roy, it seemed to Reynard, was not displeased with his progress; as for himself, he was astonished at the change which the training had wrought in him. He felt not only physically fitter, but mentally more stable; the disquieting sense of 'dissolution', the feeling that his 'identity' was about to slip from him, had become, almost, a thing of the past: it was like some degrading habit of which he had almost cured himself, and though, like a habit, it remained as a possibility at the back of his mind, the temptation to indulge it grew less and less potent as the weeks passed.

He had also, in obedience to Roy's emphatic advice, almost given up smoking. His rare indulgences were followed by such intolerable fits of guilt that the very fear of his own remorse became an effective deterrent. He found, moreover, when such lapses did occur, that he was still unable to appreciate the taste of tobacco, and this, too, helped to lessen the temptation.

Mrs Langrish, if she detected any change in him, made no comment. Reynard had wondered, for some time, whether his improved health had become noticeable to her, and so reluctant was he to reveal its true cause that he went to considerable lengths, even when at home, to conceal his sense of well-being, and even to assume on occasion his former air of languor and depression. Nor did the increasing lateness of his homecoming on his training evenings occasion any remark; indeed, it was a matter of surprise to himself that the hour of his arrival was never quite so late as he supposed. Doubtless, the fact that he was usually driven home in

Roy's car, instead of having to catch a bus, would account for this.

Scrupulous in concealing from his mother the true nature of his evening occupations, he was even more careful to keep his 'training' a secret from others. During his working-hours not a word escaped him as to his friendship with Roy; and when Roy himself paid one of his frequent visits to the bank, no slightest word or gesture on either side betrayed the close bond which united them. Reynard, indeed, adopted a brusque, almost discourteous tone towards Roy, and would sometimes silently criticize his friend for appearing too friendly.

One evening, driving up to the training-ground, Roy's manner was more eagerly intent than usual.

'We've got a surprise for you to-night,' he chuckled. 'All these things take time,' he added, with an air of mystery, 'but we're getting organized, gradually, and with the cold nights coming we'll need a little comfort.'

These mysterious words were in part explained, on their arrival at the camp, by the fact that one of the abandoned Nissen huts nearby appeared to be inhabited. Lights blazed from the windows, figures moved about the entrance, and from inside came the sound of subdued voices. Roy parked his car by the side of the hut, and with a certain pride ushered Reynard in.

The place had been transformed into a gymnasium; vaulting horses and parallel-bars had been installed, ropes and trapezes hung from the ceiling. A small area was roped off for boxing; and at one end was a trestle-table, on which was an urn of tea and a tray of sandwiches. A coke-stove in the centre supplied warmth, and in one corner were a couple of double-decker Army beds, complete with straw palliasses and blankets. A score or so of young men were already exercising: among them Reynard was almost certain that he recognized Spike Mandeville, the boxer. In a leisurely way, Roy had already begun to change into his gym-kit, and Reynard followed his example. Presently one of the men, evidently holding some kind of authority, issued a brief word of command, and the rest, including Roy and Reynard formed up in three ranks. Half-an hour's strenuous P.T. ensued, followed by twenty minutes' squad-drill; afterwards, the men dispersed to other occupations, some to the parallel bars, some to the ropes, others to the boxing ring.

'We'll have a bit of sparring,' Roy suggested, and shortly afterwards Reynard found himself detailed for instruction with the redoubtable Spike Mandeville. Spike proved to be an admirable instructor, and Reynard was glad of the opportunity to improve his form: the soldier, however, found a certain difficulty in controlling his strength, and once or twice Reynard had an unwelcome taste of the famous left-hook, for which Spike afterwards apologized handsomely enough.

'Thinkin' of signing on, are you, mate?' Spike queried later, over a cup of tea. 'Might do a lot worse – the way things are going, you don't get a proper chance in Civvy Street; we'll all be back sooner or later, so it pays you to get back while the going's good – that's what I say, anyway.'

Most of the other men to whom Reynard spoke appeared of the same mind; some, like Spike, were already enlisted, and doing a part-time job as instructors; the rest, like himself, were undergoing preliminary training. Many of them were strongly built, and looked like seasoned soldiers; several, by an odd coincidence, were tattooed in the same manner as Spike, with a snake embracing a drawn sword.

At the end of the evening silence was called for a special announcement. This was delivered by the man (perhaps a sergeant or warrant-officer) who had conducted the P.T., and who appeared to be a kind of unofficial master-of-ceremonies.

'Listen, you chaps,' he began. 'I've been asked by the O.C. to give out the following announcement: 'All personnel who have completed six weeks' training by the sixteenth of November" – that's next Monday week – "will be considered eligible for enlistment or re-enlistment on a regular engagement on the first of December. Qualified personnel desirous of taking this opportunity should report to the recruiting-centre, Department X.19, not later than 16.30 hours on that date. Identity-cards, ration-cards and shaving-kit should be carried".'

The announcer paused, and there was a round of clapping and a few cat-calls.

'Well,' he added, 'that applies to all of you chaps – so now you've got the griff. I'll read the announcement over once again, so as you can't make no mistakes.'

He repeated the announcement at dictation-speed; there were more cat-calls, more whistles, another round of clapping.

'All right, lads,' the announcer concluded. 'Remember, you're not forced to sign on: there's still time to change your minds.' (Here a burst of laughter interrupted him.) 'But if you take my advice,' he continued, 'you won't have no second thoughts about it. It's a grand life, and you'll have a grand job to do: and don't forget one more thing – if you sign on now, you've got bloody good chances of promotion. So roll up on the first of next month, and don't forget your ration-cards.'

There was another burst of laughter; and with the speech over, the party began to break up: there was a hustle for clothes, a last-minute fatigue-party cleared away the tea-things, the gym-equipment was straightened up, and, lastly, the Tilley-lamps extinguished, and the stove doused with the remains of the tea. With a surpising rapidity the assembly dispersed, and soon Reynard found himself in Roy's car, driving back towards Priors-holt.

During the journey Reynard was rather silent. Like the rest, he was eligible for re-enlistment in a little over three weeks' time. The announcement had come as a shock to him: he had vaguely supposed that the training-period would continue for some months yet, or perhaps indefinitely; he was unprepared for the necessity of making such a rapid decision. True, there was no compulsion about it: yet he felt that he had, without any spoken pledge, committed himself to a regular engagement. Ever since the first night at the Roman Camp – or, for that matter, ever since his first meeting with Roy – he had been subconsciously aware of the fact; but he had contrived, by a subtle mental duplicity, to avoid, up till now, the full realization of his obligation. It would be easy enough not to turn up on the first of December; but he knew that if he failed to do so he would never be able to look Roy in the face again. He would feel ashamed every time his friend came into the bank; further intercourse would be impossible: and he would relapse, before long, into the old unhealthy life, his 'sense of dissolution', always lying in wait, would once more overwhelm him. No, he would have to go through with it now; there must be, as the announcer had said, no 'second thoughts'.

'Well,' said Roy, almost as though Reynard had spoken aloud, 'have you made up your mind yet?'

Reynard glanced round at him, startled. They were ap-proaching the village; in a few minutes Roy would have gone, and he would be left to face the problem by himself. The prospect of coming to a decision alone, without the heartening presence of his friend, was suddenly unbearable. He must make up his mind immediately, once and for all, while Roy was still at his side, before the car pulled up. But he remained silent, his mind a blank, cursing his native indecision.

'Well?' Roy repeated, quietly, at his side. 'Are you coming in with us?'

Suddenly it was as though a veil were lifted in his mind: the accumulated dishonesties, the false assumptions, the intellectual short-cuts of the last few weeks were suddenly revealed to him. For one lucid instant he realized how abysmally ignorant he was of Roy's 'scheme', and of the whole mysterious business; he was aware, with a prickling embarrassment, of how he had persuaded himself, for very shame of his own ignorance, into a false and 'wishful' comprehension; he remembered the hints, the spoken words, the obscure gestures which, with an incorrigible dishonesty, he had pretended to understand. For the moment, he hated Roy – hated him for his overweening self-importance and for his arrogant air of authority; hated him, even, for his crude, animal vitality; hated him above all for his ability to exact the irrational and degrading personal loyalty which his wolfish pride demanded.

The car pulled up in the lane outside the house; once again Roy spoke.

'Well?' he said laconically.

Reynard made no move. From the house, the warm light shone out upon the garden-shrubs, the half-open gate. Suddenly Reynard turned, despairingly, towards his friend.

'Don't you realize,' he burst out, 'that I don't know – I've never known – *what all this is about*? I've taken your word for everything – the training-scheme, the "emergency" you're always talking about, the war or whatever it is – and you've never really explained a single thing. Why have I got to enlist? What's the meaning of it all? Can't you tell me the truth, for once, so that I can understand?'

Roy had sat in silence during Reynard's outburst. Now he turned and faced his friend, the familiar, vague smile parting his lips.

'What's the trouble this time?' he queried, half-laughing.

'The trouble?' Reynard almost shouted. 'The *trouble*, as you call it, is just that I don't know what the hell you're all up to, or what I'm up to myself, for that matter. This training, all this talk of enlisting, and learning boxing, and – and. . . .'

'Yes – and what?' Roy encouraged, as Reynard's voice broke down.

'Oh, *you* know – you know as well as I do.' Reynard was almost sobbing: he could have struck the placid, grinning face at his side.

'Exactly,' Roy retorted, calmly. 'I know as well as you do – you've said it. Doesn't it strike you that if *I* know as well as *you* do, then probably *you* know as well as *I* do? It seems logical, doesn't it?'

Reynard was silent; the moment's lucidity had passed, the veil had fallen again. He sat back, exhausted: aware that he had made a fool of himself, and all to no purpose; aware also, with a sense of fatality that gripped him like a physical spasm, that he was still faced by the necessity of making up his mind.

'Doesn't it?' Roy insisted. His voice was gentle, persuasive, and still held a hint of laughter.

'Doesn't what?' Reynard murmured, wearily.

'Oh, never mind – you're tired. It was a bit strenuous, to-night. Why don't you lay off for a night or two? It doesn't do to overdo it, you know. And it's no earthly use worrying about these things – you'll only make yourself ill, and have to go sick, and we can't spare a good chap like you. Remember, you've got to be fit by December the first.'

The veil lifted for a moment.

'Roy, tell me for God's sake – *what does it all mean?*'

Reynard felt Roy's hand close over his: the pressure was oddly disquieting, like the sudden touch of an animal in the dark.

'Listen, Reynard: I'll tell you – and no bullshit; cross my heart, honest Injun and all the rest of it.' He paused, his grip tightening upon Reynard's fingers.

'Well?' Reynard muttered.

'Do you really want the truth? All right, then – the truth is that *nobody* knows. *I* don't know, the O.C. doesn't know – no more than the man-in-the-street. You read the papers –' ('I don't,' Reynard interjected, feebly, but Roy disregarded him) – 'You know as much about the general set-up as we do. The point is, we *do* know the other lot's up to *something*, but we don't know exactly what; we even suspect – though we aren't sure – what territories they've got their eye on; at the moment, though, we can't do a thing – our hands are tied. We've simply got to trust the boss – that's to say, our immediate superiors; I trust the O.C., the O.C. trusts Command H.Q., and so on. It's obvious you can't have a lot of careless talk – that's why this new battalion's got to be raised more or less secretly. I suppose the other lot's doing just the same as we are. . . .'

'But who *are* the other lot?' Reynard cut in.

Roy laughed shortly.

'I only wish I knew,' he replied. 'If we knew that, we'd be well away. All we know is they're up there, and we've got to be ready when the balloon goes up.'

Reynard felt suddenly immensely tired.

'I must get indoors,' he said, in a flat voice. 'I'm late already.'

'So am I, by Jove,' Roy exclaimed. 'It's time I was back in Glamber – there's a mess-meeting at half-past nine. . . . Well, see you to-morrow.' As Reynard got out of the car Roy suddenly held out his hand. Reynard took it reluctantly.

'Look here, old boy,' Roy muttered, and for once there was no trace of a smile on his face. 'I'm serious about this: I want to know for certain if you're coming in with us. I don't want to bounce you into a promise, or anything – not immediately, anyway. But I'd like to know soon. Could you let me know to-morrow, do you think?'

Reynard considered for a moment, clasping his friend's hand; then, once again, he lifted his eyes to meet the dark questioning gaze.

'Yes,' he replied. 'I'll let you know to-morrow.'

CHAPTER EIGHT

The Darkening Land

On the following morning Reynard awoke with a headache and a slight sore throat. He had slept badly, and from the moment of waking he was oppressed by the thought of his last night's promise to Roy; the physical symptoms seemed a kind of extension of his mental unease. True, he had not finally committed himself to an early enlistment; but he had promised Roy a decision by this evening, and he knew that, once in the presence of his friend, he would be powerless to resist the influence of that vital and over-bearing personality.

During the morning his oppression increased; so, too, did his physical malaise. By lunch time it was obvious that he would be unfit for the evening's activities; it would be better, surely, to put off Roy altogether. The decision to do so brought him a profound relief: if he could avoid meeting Roy he would be able to postpone the fulfilment of his previous night's promise. The sense of relief, the hope of respite, were not, in fact, consciously formulated; they remained latent: though he was half-aware, with an obscure sense of shame, of his own self-deception. . . . It was sufficient excuse (so it seemed to him) that he was genuinely unwell: Roy would surely understand this; indeed, he had himself suggested, only yesterday, that he should 'lay-off' for a night or two . . .

To cancel his date with Roy, however, proved less easy than he had supposed. The best method, he decided, would be to telephone to the barracks, but once having made up his mind to do so, a host of minor difficulties beset him. In the first place, it was obvious that he couldn't ring up from the bank; the nearest public telephone box proved to be out of order; and when at length he discovered another, more distant call-box, he found that he had failed to retrieve his two pennies from the previous one. Next, he found difficulty in obtaining change; by the time he had succeeded in doing so, the call-box was occupied, and a further delay ensued. At last, entering the call-box, he proceeded to look up Roy's number in the directory, but here again a difficulty presented itself, for, never having rung up Roy before, he was uncertain of his friend's exact unit and location. There appeared to be two battalions of the regiment stationed at the barracks; and he was embarrassingly aware that he had forgotten (or perhaps never bothered to ask) which battalion Roy belonged to. His first call was unsuccessful; nobody had heard of Captain Archer. 'Try the second battalion,' the voice on the line suggested. Reynard obeyed; the reply came after some delay, indistinctly: no, there was no Captain Archer with the second battalion. Did he mean *Major* Archer?

Reynard hesitated: perhaps, he thought, Roy had been promoted; it was quite possible that he had failed to notice the fact last night. Finally, he asked to speak to Major Archer. After further delay, a new voice came over the wire.

'Hullo! Major Archer here – who's that speaking?'

To Reynard, the voice appeared to be Roy's, though he could not, owing to some obstruction on the line, be quite certain.

'Hullo,' he replied cautiously. 'This is Reynard Langrish. I rang up to tell you I've got a touch of 'flu, and shan't be able to turn up to-night.'

A fusillade of crackling came from the other end; at last, the voice emerged again.

'What name did you say?'

'Langrish,' Reynard repeated. 'L-a-n-g-r-i-s-h.'

'*Langrish?* Sorry, I don't know the name. I'm afraid you've got the wrong bloke. This is Roy Archer here. What's that? I can't hear you – what's the name again? No, I'm sorry – I don't know it. You must have got the wrong number.'

There was a click: Major Roy Archer had hung up the receiver.

Reynard left the box, feeling suddenly weak and ill. He sat down for a moment on a seat by the bus stop, trying to master the trembling which shook his limbs. His mind was inextricably confused: had he spoken to Roy or had he not? The voice, suspiciously like his friend's, had distinctly said 'Roy Archer': was it possible, then, that there were two Roy Archers? Or had Roy, after all, failed to catch his name? Weary, bewildered, and feeling increasingly ill, Reynard left his seat and began to walk back towards the bank. A further possible explanation occurred to him: perhaps the pretence of being 'strangers', which himself and Roy had sustained for so long, was now to be imposed, not only in the bank, but outside it as well? Surely, if this were the case, Roy would have mentioned it: yet one couldn't, Reynard decided, feel altogether certain on this point, for the tacit concealing of their relationship in the bank had never been explicitly referred to by either of them.

Feeling too sick to eat any lunch, Reynard returned to his work; unluckily, the bank was busier than usual, and at closing time it was evident that nobody would be able to get away till late in the afternoon. Once again, Reynard was half aware of an ignoble sense of relief: if he were forced to remain for long enough at work, Roy would no doubt get tired of waiting for him. . . . Perhaps it was partly this half-admitted hope which caused him to work more slowly and laboriously than usual; partly, no doubt, he was impeded by his increasing feverishness. For one reason or another, it was half-past six before he left the bank: far later than usual, and much too late (he decided) to make it worth while to look for Roy.

Leaving the bank he started out, from habit, to walk down the High Street to the bus stop by the Town Hall. Suddenly he turned aside and, cutting down a side street, made for the next stop on the bus-route; he had remembered that he needed some new razor-blades, and that the shop where he usually dealt lay in this direction. The thought that Roy might still be waiting for him, by the Town Hall bus-station, stirred uneasily at the back of his mind; but he ignored it, assuring himself that he did indeed require razor blades, and that a slightly longer walk than usual might do him good.

By the time he reached the bus-stop it was almost dark. Seeing a tobacconist's shop nearby, he decided to break with his resolutions, and purchase some cigarettes. With a curious sense of degradation, he bought a packet of twenty Goldflake and a box of matches, and, while he waited for the bus, took out a cigarette and lit it. The tobacco was more tasteless than usual, owing, no doubt, to his feverish condition; he flung the cigarette away and waited impatiently on the pavement-edge, watching for the bus.

As he waited, a car passed by, slowly enough to catch his attention. The car was suddenly familiar; a fit of trembling seized him and he was about to turn away; something deterred him, however, and before he could make a move the driver had turned his head sideways and was looking him full in the eyes.

It was Roy Archer.

Reynard stared back at him, half-hypnotized by the dark familiar gaze. It was only for an instant; the face turned away, the car sped forwards towards the changing traffic-lights. A moment later, Reynard's bus pulled up at the pavement, and he climbed on to it. Sick, trembling, scarcely aware of his surroundings, he took his seat and fumbled for his ticket; paralysed by a fear such as he had never known or believed possible: the fear that he might be going insane.

For Roy had *stared through him*; not by the slightest sign had he betrayed that he was aware of Reynard's presence. The weeks of comradeship, the 'training-scheme', the teas and drinks at the 'Valiant Trooper', the 'gymnasium' on the downs – all these were as nothing, vague memories as remote as those of childhood, or of some shadowy pre-existence. Perhaps, thought Reynard desperately, they had never happened: perhaps his whole complex relationship with Roy was an illusion; yet he could not believe it – remembering Roy's handclasp, his familiar turns of speech and his friendly, fatuous smile.

'What's up, mate – feeling queer?' the conductor asked, as he took Reynard's ticket.

'I'm not feeling too good – a touch of 'flu,' Reynard muttered, indistinctly. 'I'll be all right . . .'

He straightened himself and stared fixedly out of the window, forcing his disordered mind into some semblance of coherence. The bus gave a lurch and, gathering speed as it approached the town's outskirts, rolled onwards at a steady pace, past the allotments, the sports-ground and the new building-estate, towards the darkening land beyond.

CHAPTER NINE

Like Some Unhappy Ghost

Reynard's attack of influenza (for such it proved to be) kept him from the bank for the next ten days. For forty-eight hours he was acutely ill, and it seemed that some dangerous complication might supervene; gradually, however, after the fourth day, his temperature dropped and he made a slow recovery.

His illness induced in him a curious vagueness about recent events, and for some days the memory of Roy and, indeed, of the whole period of their acquaintance, remained latent, ill-defined as the memory of a dream. It was his mother, as it happened, who unwittingly roused him to full recollection. During the first phase of his illness he had been slightly delirious and, according to Mrs Langrish, had incessantly repeated the name of Roy Archer; he had appeared, she said, to be engaged in some interminable telephone conversation in which he was trying to convince Captain (or sometimes Major) Archer of his own identity. She only mentioned this, Mrs Langrish added, since she had wondered if it were anything important connected with business, about which it might be advisable to remind him.

In an instant, the whole bewildering sequence of that last day in Glamber returned to him; yet now, at this distance, the actual events seemed curiously unimportant. The quality of nightmare which, at the time, had seemed to pervade them, could be discounted by the fact that he had been sickening for a severe illness. Even the strange telephone conversation had probably had some quite simple explanation; and Roy's apparent ignoring of him at the bus-stop could be easily accounted for by the slight myopia from which Reynard knew his friend to be a sufferer.

'It was nothing of the least importance,' he assured his mother.

'I tried to ring up Roy Archer that day – the day I was taken ill – and couldn't get through. You remember Roy – Captain Archer – he came in one night to ask the way, and then took me over to Larchester, to see some boxing.'

'Boxing?' Mrs Langrish queried. 'I don't remember anything about boxing.'

'Well, you remember Roy, then – Roy Archer,' Reynard insisted. It seemed to him suddenly important that his mother should recall the occasion.

'Carter, did you say?' she dubiously asked.

'No, not Carter – Archer,' Reynard repeated impatiently. 'Roy Archer.'

His mother shook her head.

'I can't say I remember anyone of that name,' she murmured.

'But you must remember,' Reynard insisted. 'It was only about six weeks ago – he came in on that stormy night, the night the tile blew off, you remember? And he recognized father's photograph.'

Mrs Langrish continued to look dubious; and the more Reynard insisted, the more difficult did it seem to her to cast her mind back to the night of the storm.

'But surely you must remember him,' Reynard exclaimed irritably. 'We don't have so many visitors.'

'I do remember somebody – but it was a long time ago – someone from the bank. . . .?'

'Well, yes – he's one of our customers.'

'A strange man, I remember thinking,' Mrs Langrish said, musingly.

'Not particularly strange I shouldn't have thought. A fairly ordinary sort of chap – officer type, rather. Fair-haired, tallish – he parts his hair in the middle. You remember now, surely?'

Mrs Langrish shook her head.

'Tall, did you say?' she asked.

'Yes, fairly tall.' Reynard repeated his description, for, with seeming perversity, his mother's deafness appeared to have become more impenetrable than usual. Finally, after he had described Roy's appearance a second and even a third time, it seemed still a matter of doubt whether she had entirely understood; nor could she be persuaded to admit that she recalled anybody answering exactly to his description.

Several times Reynard returned to the attack: his mother's lapse of memory became a mild obsession with him during the period of his convalescence. Finally, he let the matter drop; such lapses were common enough, as he knew – Mrs Langrish, after all, was over seventy – and he was unwilling to pester her unnecessarily over such a trivial affair. None the less, her complete inability to remember his friend afflicted him with a lingering disquiet; becoming linked in his mind with the unsatisfactory telephone call, and Roy's blank unrecognizing stare at the bus-stop.

On the whole, Reynard was not displeased when the doctor allowed him to return to work; he had been glad of the rest, but the atmosphere of his home, always rather oppressive, had become almost intolerably so during the last days of his convalescence. His mother's lapses of memory, her increasing deafness, began to irritate him past bearing; and his return to the bank had for him a quality of almost holiday excitement.

It was a grey chilly day in mid-November when he set out for Glamber for the first time. The last leaves were falling from the almost naked trees, and the town itself, when he reached it, had a singularly deserted air, as though the population had fled before some pestilence or threat of war.

At the bank business was fairly slack, fortunately for Reynard, who found some difficulty at first in settling down to the laborious routine. Throughout that first day he found himself constantly on the alert lest Roy Archer should make an appearance: glancing up every time the swing-doors were thrust open, half-hoping and half-fearing to see the tall athletic figure stride across to the counter. For reasons which he hardly cared to analyse, the prospect unnerved him; yet the mere sight of his friend would, he felt, be in some way reassuring, confirming the reality of a relationship which, since his illness, had taken on a curiously insubstantial and dream-like quality.

Roy, however, did not visit the bank that day. When the time came to start for home, Reynard walked down to his usual bus-stop by the Town Hall; half-hoping, half-fearing that Roy's car would be parked in its habitual place. Not surprisingly, neither Roy nor his car were in sight; it was hardly likely that he should be aware of Reynard's recovery since he had never, in the first place, been informed of his illness. Reynard, unreasonably hoping, was as unreasonably disappointed by his friend's absence; yet with his disappointment was mingled a certain sense of relief. If Roy didn't choose to turn up again at the bus-stop, there wasn't much he could do about it. It had occurred to him, during his convalescence, that he might write to him, but his illness had made him lethargic, and in any case he remained uncertain of Roy's actual rank and of his battalion, not to mention his correct address.

Yet as he rode home on the bus, Reynard continued to speculate as to what methods he could adopt to renew relations with his friend. He was unwilling to risk another telephone call; nor did it seem very likely that Roy would turn up again at the usual meeting place. Doubtless, he would visit the bank, but it was by no means certain that he would consider Reynard's illness sufficient reason for breaking the established rules of their intercourse. Yet this seemed the only hope; and Reynard determined that, on Roy's next visit, he would contrive some secret means of communication with him. He might, for instance (especially if the other clerks were occupied with customers) contrive to pass a note across the counter; or, if this failed, he might on some pretext follow Roy out of the bank.

Meanwhile, the date fixed for enlistment – December the first – was less than a fortnight ahead. The date remained, clearly printed upon Reynard's brain; but the other details of the announcement had already slipped his memory – in particular, the time and place at which recruits must present themselves. There was, he knew, no recruiting office in Glamber – the nearest one was in the county town, some thirty miles away. It was possible, of course, that some special arrangement would be made for the enlistment to take place locally, but unless he could contact Roy or some of the other people concerned, there seemed no way of finding out.

Later, walking down the lane to the village, it struck him that the night was curiously disturbed; birds squawked and chattered restlessly in the plantation, and a dog howled in some remote farm as though scenting danger. The moon, rising over the downs, glinted with a sulphurous light through a brownish pall of cloud; and the wind, chilly and rain-laden from the south-east, sighed fitfully, like some unhappy ghost, through the leafless beeches.

CHAPTER TEN

A Queer Caper

For several days Reynard waiting anxiously for Roy to visit the bank; he did not, however, appear; nor was he to be found again at the old meeting place by the Town Hall.

As the day gradually approached when he might (if he still wished) enlist in Roy's newly-raised battalion, Reynard became the prey of an extraordinary mixture of feelings. Fear predominated, a fear which gripped his bowels like a physical spasm, reminding him of his boyhood, and the terrifying prospect of going to a new school. At the same time he was half-determined, if the opportunity occurred, to offer himself as a recruit; it was not so much a conscious act of will as a kind of deep, unthinking compulsion. This hidden urge was accompanied by a peculiar emotional excitement, comparable to the vague stirrings of sexuality in an adolescent; it was linked with some idea of surrender, of abandoning himself to some experience which would probably prove unpleasant and even dangerous, but which none the less would *provide an escape*. The oppression of his home, the monotonous toil of the bank, the dull, circumscribed existence which he resented yet forced himself to tolerate – from all this, Roy Archer's strange proposals had promised some kind of release. It might be that he would merely exchange one form of oppressive routine for another; his previous service in the Army had left him with no illusions about soldiering; yet it seemed to him that any change, however unpleasant, would be welcome.

In such moods, given the chance, he would have enlisted on the spot; lacking the opportunity, lacking even the knowledge of the requisite procedure, his impulse was inhibited; the prospect of surrendering himself to the hard, uncouth, comfortless world of the soldier would fill him with sudden horror; fear gripped his bowels again; and, resuming once more his quotidian, 'commonsense' attitude, he would tell himself that his projected 'enlistment' was the act of a madman.

For a day or so at a time, this 'commonsense' mood would retain its sway over him; then some sudden word or incident would revive the irrational urge to abandon himself to the life which he dreaded yet profoundly desired.

One evening, as he left the bank, a column of soldiers marched past him down the High Street. He stood to watch them: they were in shirt-sleeve order (for the day was mild), and were evidently on their way back to camp after a strenuous route-march. As he watched, he felt once again his excitement kindle, and the old impulse reassert itself: this time, he decided, there would be no 'second thoughts'; he must find the recruiting-centre without delay, before his intention had had time to weaken.

His resolve burning within him, he walked down to the Town Hall. Once again, the old irrational hope possessed him that Roy might be waiting there. Assuring himself that his friend was nowhere to be seen, he stood for a moment, irresolute, upon the pavement. Then a sudden thought struck him: instead of waiting for the bus to Priorsholt, he crossed the road and boarded one which was just about to set off in the opposite direction. . . . Roy, it seemed, had deserted him; little more than a week remained before he must present himself for enlistment; there was only one thing to do – he must revisit the mysterious 'gymnasium' near the Roman Camp.

To discover the 'gymnasium', however, without guidance and on a dark November night, proved less easy than Reynard had expected. He left the bus at what he supposed to be the turning to the Roman Camp; he had not gone far, however, before he realized that he was on the wrong road. Retracing his steps to the main road, he walked on further, and took another turning. This appeared to be the right one, but still he couldn't be sure; on previous occasions he had always approached the 'camp' in Roy's car, and he had taken scarcely any note of the landmarks. True, he had visited the place before his acquaintance with Roy, but that was many months ago, and his visits, naturally, had been made by daylight.

He saw now, across a field, what he took to be the group of Nissen huts; and, at some risk of losing his way, he cut down a sidepath towards his objective. The huts, however, proved strangely elusive; the twilight had faded into almost-darkness since he left the main road, and a slight mist was rising over the downs. He stumbled on, barking his shins on a broken-down fence, stumbling over rabbit holes and hidden strands of barbed wire. Presently he reached what he had presumed to be the huts; to his disappointment, the buildings proved to be a group of sheds surrounding a small farm-house. There was no light in the house; a dog, however, barked fiercely as he passed, and there was a fluttering and squawking of poultry from one of the sheds.

Once beyond the farm, he found himself in more open country, and suddenly, to his joy, recognized what seemed almost certainly the plateau surrounding the Roman Camp. He fancied that he could even detect the faint outlines of the earthworks and tumuli, and hurried forward, but of the Nissen huts there seemed to be no sign whatever. He stopped to renew his sense of direction, then set off round the edge of the plateau, keeping the central eminence carefully in sight. By this means, he thought, it would be impossible to miss the huts if they were there; and after walking for another five minutes, his perseverance was rewarded.

The group of huts stood in a slight depression, a fact which doubtless made them almost invisible from even a short distance. From the window of one of them came a faint illumination; Reynard's heart leapt with sudden hope as he hurried forward and, stepping cautiously over the uneven ground, approached the dark, huddled mass of buildings. After a moment's pause, he identified the hut from which the dim light emanated and, walking boldly up to the entrance, pushed the door open and entered.

His first impression was one of bitter disappointment. The faint light of a single candle flickered in the gloom, revealing the fact that the hut was practically empty. The ropes, the bars, the vaulting-horse had gone; no visible sign remained of the 'gymnasium', and one would, in fact, have supposed that the place had been disused for many months.

Beyond the flickering candle flame Reynard could just discern what appeared to be a pile of old sacks and straw; and as he stood at the doorway, peering curiously into the dimness, he was suddenly startled by the sound of a human voice.

'Who's that?'

The words were uttered sharply, with a note of menace: coming, apparently, from the amorphous, shadowy heap beyond the candle. Reynard stepped forward and saw, sitting half-upright on the piled sacks, the figure of a man. The face was rough and unshaven, a torn, diry shirt gaped open, revealing a patch of black hair; a pair of bright, piercing eyes regarded Reynard with an alert hostility.

'Who's that? What yer want?' the voice repeated.

'I'm sorry,' Reynard answered nervously. 'I was looking – I thought. . . .'

'Yeah, who was yer lookin' for?' the man cut in roughly. 'There ain't no one here, only me, and I ain't needin' no company, see?'

'I was looking for the – the gym,' Reynard stammered, aware of the ludicrous effect which his words must produce.   ·

'Lookin' for Jim? There ain't no Jim 'ere,' the man retorted sharply.

'No, the gym – gymnasium, the training centre. I was up here a few weeks ago, the troops were using this hut for training. I thought – I wondered. . . .'

Evidently supposing Reynard to be some kind of harmless lunatic, the man's eyes became less hostile.

'Well, there ain't no troops 'ere now,' he said. 'You can look round and see, if you like. Fair startled me, you did – I thought you was a copper. Not as I've owt to fear from the coppers, but I'm on the road, see, an' I just turned in 'ere for a kip.'

'Yes, I see,' Reynard murmured, in a curiously flat voice, hardly attending to the man's words. 'I'm sorry I disturbed you.' Suddenly his attention was caught by something on the floor, near the candle. 'Are those yours?' he queried, and held up, for the tramp's inspection, a pair of Army-pattern P.T. shorts.

'Nah, they ain't mine. Must have been left 'ere by the soldiers. See here, mate,' – the voice took on suddenly a friendly, persuasive note – 'I suppose you ain't got 'arf a dollar you could spare? I'm down to me last bleedin' farthing, straight I am.'

Reynard felt in his pocket, and handed the man half a crown.

'Cor, you're a real toff – thanks a lot, chum. It's real good of you. . . . Sorry I can't help you – you must have struck the wrong spot. . . . Which way are yer travellin', anyway?'

'I'm not travelling,' Reynard muttered. He felt suddenly immensely tired, as though he had undergone some prolonged and nerve-racking physical ordeal.

'Well, you looks just about done in,' the man remarked. Suddenly he extended his left hand, to straighten the candle, from which the grease was dripping wastefully upon the floor. With an odd, hallucinatory vividness, the bare forearm presented itself to Reynard's strained and searching vision; and a sudden excitement leapt in him as he recognized, branded in the white flesh, the identical design which he remembered seeing on the arm of Spike Mandeville and several of the other men at the 'gymnasium': a blue and red serpent curled about a naked sword.

'Better sit yourself down for a bit,' the man muttered. 'You look proper seedy. I was just goin' to make a nice cup o' cocoa – you can have a drop, if you like.'

Overcome by an irresistible weakness, Reynard sat down on the piled sacks. The man rose and began to make preparations for his supper. Reynard must have dozed off, for when he was next fully conscious, his companion was holding towards him a tin mug of steaming cocoa.

' 'Ere you are, mate,' he said, with a rough kindliness.

Reynard thanked him, scarcely able to raise his voice above a whisper.

'That's all right, chum – you done me a good turn, an' I ain't one to forget it. You looks proper queer – what's that you was saying about troops and gymnasiums and all? Sounds a queer caper to me – I thought you was barmy, honest I did.'

After a drink of the cocoa, Reynard felt his strength suddenly returning. An odd sense of well-being stole over him: sitting on the piled sacks and rubble, in the deserted shell of the 'gymnasium' with a tramp for company, he felt more contented and at ease than for some time past.

'Who was it you was lookin' for?' the man repeated curiously, his coarse but not unpleasant face bending over Reynard in the dim light, inquisitive yet kindly. Reynard felt a sudden impulse to take the tramp into his confidence. There could be no harm in it; and the man himself (branded as he was with what Reynard had come to believe was the distinguishing mark of the training battalion) might possibly know something of the enlistment arrangements, or even of Roy's whereabouts.

Haltingly, with many pauses and much repetition, he began to tell his story, it must sound, he realized, like the ravings of a madman. Yet the tramp appeared, when he had grasped the main outlines, to find it intelligible and rational. Gaining confidence, Reynard told him of his illness ('I thought you looked seedy'), of Roy's disappearance, of the imminent date of enlistment.

'December the first, is it?' the man echoed. 'Well, if I was you, chum, I'd forget about it. They tried to get *me* back, but I done six years in the war – Africa, Italy, Germany and all – and I ain't doin' no more. Civvy Street's good enough for me, even bummin' around like I'm doing – there's jobs goin', for them as wants 'em, but I ain't so bloody anxious to settle down yet awhile. . . . See 'ere, mate, if you ain't got nowhere to go, you can kip 'ere – there's room enough for two.'

Reynard thought of the dark walk back to the main road, the journey to Glamber, the long ride home to Priorsholt: the tramp's offer seemed extraordinarily tempting. His fatigue oppressed him like a dead weight: merely to raise his arm to look at his watch seemed an intolerable effort.

'Well, what about it?' his strange host repeated.

'All right,' Reynard agreed weakly. 'I'll stay.'

'O.K., chum – we'll keep each other warm,' the tramp promised, hospitably. The sacks and straw were rearranged; Reynard took off his coat and tie, and the two men, having first extinguished the candle, lay down side by side.

For a while they talked, disjointedly, in short snatches: once again, sleepily, Reynard raised the question of his enlistment, half-hoping that his companion might yet give him the information he required. But the tramp seemed to know nothing of the recruiting office, or of the procedure for enlistment. Gradually, Reynard's waking thoughts merged into a series of dreams: once again he was stumbling across the darkening fields, in search of the hut; once again he pushed the door open and saw the single candle and the dim figure beyond: but this time the man who greeted him was not the tramp, but Spike Mandeville, the boxer. . . . Later he dreamed that he had returned home and found his mother sitting in the kitchen; she had her back to him, and it was some moments before he was able to attract her attention. When at last he did so, and she turned towards him, he was horrified to see that her face was disfigured by some loathsome disease. . . . He woke sweating, with a sense of peculiar degradation, aware of the heavy body lying closely against his own, and of the tramp's breath falling warmly upon his exposed face.

CHAPTER ELEVEN

The First of December

When Reynard woke again it was to find the grey, wintry daylight streaming in at the hut windows; he was surprised, on turning his head, to find that his bedfellow had disappeared. He looked at his watch: it was a quarter-past eight – he would have to hurry if he were to get to the bank on time. He rose stiffly from the improvised bed and went outside: half expecting to find the tramp still lurking somewhere in the area of the camp. There was no sign of him, however, and he seemed, as Reynard observed when he re-entered the hut, to have removed all traces of his occupation.

The morning was chilly and grey, threatening rain; as Reynard started on his walk to the main road, a pall of mist drifted over the high plateau, obscuring the outlines of the Roman Camp, enveloping the huts themselves, so that his night's adventure began to take on for him the unreality of a dream. Reaching the road at last, he was fortunate enough to catch an early bus to the town; his first thought on his arrival was to get a shave, and after some search he found a barber's shop already open for business. It was not till the barber had shaved him, and he had emptied his pockets of his remaining small change, that it occurred to him to feel in his breast pocket for his note-case.

The pocket was empty.

He was not unduly surprised at the loss; the tramp's early departure had been suspicious. Drearily he realized that he had only himself to blame for his misfortune. Standing in the empty street, outside the hairdresser's shop, he was overwhelmed by a sudden, desolate unhappiness: not for the mere theft of his money (which he could easily afford, as it happened) but for a greater and more irreparable loss. He recalled, with a visionary clarity, the

strange encounter in the hut: the tramp's rough kindness, his offer
of the cocoa and a 'kip', the sudden birth of trust and a brief,
transient affection from their shared wretchedness. The trust, even
the affection, had been genuine; of this Reynard was still profoundly convinced; yet they had not been able to survive the night;
dawn had brought corruption, the precocious flower had withered
in the bud.

A quarter of an hour remained before Reynard need arrive at the
bank; this he employed in telephoning to a neighbour at Priorsholt,
and leaving a message for his mother, explaining that he had been
kept late at the bank and had accepted an offer of a bed in the town.
The thought of his mother waiting up for him on the previous
night, with a meal prepared and his bed made ready, filled him
with an unaccustomed pity for her: and he resolved (as he had
resolved on many a previous occasion) to devote more of his time
and attention to her welfare; yet even as he made this resolution,
his brain had begun to occupy itself once again (and without any
awareness of contradiction) with the problem of his imminent
'enlistment'. Once again he cast his mind back to the previous
night, recalling how he had outlined, for the tramp's benefit, the
confused events of the last weeks; oddly, the man had seemed to
half-apprehend his story; had almost admitted that he, too, had
known something of the mysterious 'battalion'. Or had he merely
been 'humouring' his visitor, perhaps with a view to gaining his
confidence? However this might be, there remained the fact (of
more material significance than mere words) that he had borne
upon his arm the brand of Roy's followers – the snake and the
sword.

The day passed, and still Roy did not appear at the bank. On the
following morning it occurred to Reynard that there was, after all,
an easy way of discovering whether Roy was still in the neighbourhood or not. All he had to do was to find out whether Captain
Archer still had an account at the bank, or whether it had been
transferred elsewhere.

Mentioning the matter casually to Ted Garnett, Reynard found
that Captain Archer ('but he's a Major now,' said the snobbish
young clerk) had, in fact, transferred his account some weeks ago
to the branch in the county town. This discovery had, for Reynard,
an immediate significance: if Roy were now stationed at X —, it
seemed likely that the enlistments of December the first would be
taking place there, presumably at the combined recruiting centre.

What was he to do? December the first fell on a Tuesday; it would mean asking for a day off from the bank, which would not be easy unless he could give a good reason. If he were to act openly, and reveal his intention to the manager, he would have to give proper notice; and supposing, having done so, that he failed to find the recruiting centre, or were to be rejected? The whole affair bristled with difficulties; the best plan, Reynard decided, would be to ring up on the Tuesday morning and plead illness; he could then take a bus over to X — and, if his attempt were unsuccessful, he could return to the bank on the following day without too many questions being asked.

As the end of the month approached, however, Reynard found himself less and less willing to make the journey to the county town; for one thing, he still could not remember the details of time and place, as they had been announced that night at the 'gymnasium'. To assume, because Roy had transferred his account to X —, that the enlistments were to take place there, was the merest guess-work. If only he could remember that announcement! He racked his brains, but without success; so far as he could recall, the announcer had mentioned some special office or department, referring to it by what was probably some kind of code or cypher; but the actual formula used continued to elude him.

In Glamber, during the walk to and from the bank, and in the lunch hour, he kept a careful watch on the crowded pavements, hoping to recognize the face of one or another of the men with whom he had trained at the Roman Camp. On one occasion he did catch sight of a young man who seemed familiar, and followed him for some distance, only to fight shy, at the last moment, of accosting him. One evening, too, as he passed the open door of a public-house, he could have sworn that he saw the figure of Spike Mandeville standing at the bar; but once again his shyness inhibited him from entering and making himself known.

The weather turned unusually cold and unpleasant during the next few days; with some idea, perhaps, of hardening himself against Army life, in the event of his enlisting, Reynard took to going for long walks in the evenings, forcing himself to make the effort despite his fatigue, and stoically regardless of drenching rain and icy winds.

On Saturday afternoon, the twenty-eighth of November, he set off for a longer walk than usual. The wind had dropped and the rain, for the moment, abated; the afternoon was still, with a curious quality of deadness: life seemed to have ebbed away from the woods and fields, no bird or animal stirred, and the lingering hedgerow weeds were pinched and withered by the recent frosts. Remembering Roy's cryptic remarks, and haunted once again by memories of his childhood, he found himself walking in a south-easterly direction towards the uncharted region known as Clambercrown. Leaving the village by a narrow, tree-bordered lane, he climbed to the brow of the valley, where the lane skirted a large beech plantation. As was his habit, when walking in this direction, he cut through the plantation, taking a narrow path winding between the beech boles and partly overgrown with low bushes. Here and there he had to step carefully, for the bushes and creepers had in several places overgrown the slit trenches dug by troops during the war and never filled in. The plantation had in fact formed a reserve position for an anti-aircraft battery, stationed in the local manor house; it had never, however, been occupied, being intended only for use in the event of a retreat before invading forces.

Nearer the centre of the copse the path broadened, and here the bare chalk was visible beneath the undergrowth. A series of curious humps, like tumuli, surrounded the central space: they were, as a matter of fact, dugouts, and on closer inspection their entrances were revealed – openings in the piled chalk, half concealed now by the autumnal drift of beech leaves. Above the largest of these, nailed to a beech bole, was a roughly painted board bearing the words: OTHER RANKS SLEEPING QUARTERS.

The abandoned, never-occupied 'camp' had a peculiarly desolate air, commemorating as it did a disaster which had never occurred; and the hollow mounds, half buried by their drifts of leaves, had, in spite of their desolation, an odd air of expectancy, as though their disuse were merely temporary. As Reynard walked through the wood an aeroplane passed overhead; and its throbbing, hypnotic note seemed to press like a palpable weight upon the still air between the beeches.

Suddenly he paused, by the largest of the dugouts, possessed by a recurrent curiosity. Often, in passing here before, he had felt an impulse to explore one of these curious underground habitations; but he had never yet brought himself to do so. Chiefly it was sheer laziness: it seemed hardly worth the effort of stepping aside and stooping beneath the low lintel of the dug-out 'door'. There could be nothing, after all, of any interest: a drift of beech leaves beneath an arch of chalk; perhaps an empty tin or two. . . . Yet his mild curiosity persisted, and was renewed again to-day. It was an easy enough whim to satisfy – he had only to take a couple of steps off the path, and another step downwards into the piled beech mast; but the effort, trivial as it was, seemed once again too great. It was absurd, he told himself, to dirty his shoes unnecessarily, merely for the sake of standing, for an instant, entombed beneath the chalky floor of the wood.

To-day, however, he paused longer than usual by the large dugout. Should he or should he not go in and explore it? The question seemed fraught, on this occasion, with an absurdly disproportionate gravity. He stood by the entrance, beneath the motionless, dripping trees, intolerably aware of the conflict between the positive and negative poles of his being. The magnetic 'pull' of each pole seemed almost exactly balanced against the other, so as to produce a complete inhibition of his will. It seemed to him, indeed, as he stood there, that he had no will left: the power even of physical movement had deserted him, he was rooted to the chalky woodland floor as firmly as the beeches themselves. This, he thought, was precisely what it must feel like to be a beech tree; and once again he felt the familiar process beginning – the centrifugal dispersal of identity, the 'unbecoming' of his very self. The sensation produced in him a sense of profound hopelessness: he would never, he supposed, discover the mysterious recruiting centre, perhaps never see Roy again; nothing remained for him, now, but the monotonous, circumscribed life which he hated, but from which there seemed no prospect of escape.

He had lately taken to regular smoking again, and now lit a cigarette. The tobacco was as tasteless as ever; with a gesture of disgust he flung the cigarette away and walked on. Leaving the plantation, he traversed an area of parkland, crossed the railway, and took a path leading between high untrimmed hedges towards the hilly woods which bounded the horizon. It was some time since he had walked up this way, and he was aware of slight changes in the landscape: here some trees had been felled, here a few acres of pasture had been ploughed up. He noticed, also, one or two other, less easily explicable features: the edge of one field was barricaded by an elaborate barbed-wire entanglement and, a little farther on, a series of trenches had been dug in a copse. Possibly the trenches and the barbed wire were relics of the war; yet he could not remember that they had been there last time he came this way.

He walked on, doggedly, through the drenched, leafless wood-lands. The aeroplane which he had heard in the plantation still seemed to be circling overhead, though too high to be visible: its persistent hum became the very voice of the afternoon, so that he ceased, after a while, to notice it. Presently he passed a small farmhouse: a soldier was leaning against the gate, and stared watchfully at Reynard as he passed. To Reynard, the sight of the khaki-clad figure was faintly disquieting; doubtless the soldier was on leave, but somehow this explanation didn't seem quite adequate.

Half-a-mile further on the woods came to an end, and the track crossed a high plateau of pasture-land. To the left, the country dipped away into a valley; beyond lay the wooded hills which concealed the vague, indeterminate territory of Clambercrown. To reach them would mean another hour's walk, and Reynard decided to turn back. As he did so, his attention was caught by what appeared to be a cluster of bell-tents near where the woods began on the farther side of the valley, but the evening mists were already rising, and it was impossible clearly to distinguish objects at such a distance. The 'tents' were possibly small haystacks; it was certainly not worth a further three-miles walk to investigate them.

The aeroplane droned persistently overhead as Reynard retraced his steps through the woods. As he passed the farmhouse, he noticed the soldier leaning out of an upper window and regarding him as watchfully as ever; at a second glance, however, it struck him that the face was not, after all, that of the soldier whom he had seen before. Indeed, there was no resemblance: the first man had been clean-shaven, this one had a moustache and wore his hair parted in the middle. It was odd, thought Reynard, that two of a family should be on leave together; yet this seemed the only reasonable explanation.

The week-end passed, and on Monday Reynard returned to the bank. Business was unusually heavy, and it was evident that Tuesday would also be a busy day; it would scarcely be possible to ask for the day off, unless for some very urgent reason. Reynard found his mental processes assuming a familiar ambivalence; he had come to realize, at last, that his 'enlistment', due for to-morrow, was an impossibility; yet he continued to think and act as though it were not only possible, but inevitable. He had no idea how to find the recruiting centre; he was, moreover, by this time, half-inclined to believe that the whole business had been some elaborate joke on the part of Roy Archer. Yet, against all reason, his faith persisted.

He slept little on the Monday night. There seemed to be an unusual number of aeroplanes in the neighbourhood: their low, throbbing drone persisted throughout the night, haunting Reynard with the recollection of his walk on the previous Saturday.

The dawn came at last, sunless and grey: the morning of Tuesday, the first of December. Reynard rose as usual, cooked his breakfast, and started out for the bank. He felt unpleasantly tired after his restless night, but his mind was unusually calm. At the bank, he worked with his normal efficiency until half-past twelve, at which hour he was accustomed to go out for lunch.

To-day, however, instead of making as usual for the Shamrock Tea-rooms, he walked down to the Town Hall. If some last-minute hope had entered his mind that he might encounter Roy Archer, the hope was doomed to disappointment. As he stood by the bus-stop, a Priorsholt bus drew up, and he experienced a violent impulse to play truant, and surprise his mother by arriving home for an early tea. His impulse seemed curiously associated with and centred upon a metal plate which was affixed to the back of the bus; this bore an obscure inscription in official cypher – probably some code-reference to the route covered by the bus, or to its location at the Depot of the Glamber Road-Car Company. For some reason the black lettering impressed itself upon Reynard with an extra-ordinary vividness, though he could not, at the moment, think of any adequate reason for this. The bus, he noticed, was unusually crowded for the time of day – mostly with young men; probably they were workers coming off some early shift. Reluctantly, he turned away, and made his way back towards the Shamrock Tea-rooms. The fact that he had resisted his truant impulse set up in his mind a nagging sense of guilt. There was nothing whatever to feel guilty about; indeed, he should have felt, if anything, a sense of moral victory; yet the feeling persisted, increasingly, throughout the afternoon.

As he expected, work kept him late, and it was already five o'clock when he started for home. He found that he could think quite calmly and detachedly, now, about his 'enlistment'; he had done his best, after all, and if he had failed to keep what he still, at times, thought of as his 'promise' to Roy, it was through no lack of willingness on his part. Yet now that the day was nearly over, he could not help feeling a certain relief that he was still in possession of his freedom.

At home, all was as usual. Mrs Langrish prepared the evening meal, and afterwards Reynard sat down at the piano and played a Mozart sonata and some Debussy preludes of which his mother, before her deafness, had been particularly fond. Later, feeling the need of fresh air, he went out for a short walk. Almost without thinking, he turned up the lane which he had taken on the previous Saturday; the night was windless, and a fine rain fell; once again, he was aware of a sense of deadness brooding upon the country-side. It was the ebb of the seasonal tide: in another month or so the first shoots would pierce the beech-mast, birds sing in the dusk; but this was the dead season, life lurked underground, in icebound darkness, without sound or movement.

At the top of the lane Reynard turned, as usual, into the copse; suddenly a series of painful pricks in his calves and thighs made him start backwards; there was a ripping and tearing of cloth, and, striking a match, he saw that he had walked straight into a newly-erected fence of barbed wire. His trousers were torn, his legs painfully scratched; trembling with shock and with a sudden passionate anger, he stepped back on to the path; he would have sworn aloud, but a peculiar scruple kept him silent: for in that moment, he was convinced that he had not been alone in the plantation – somebody or something had been present, watchful and listening, among the drenched leafless trees.

As he walked down the lane, the recurrent hum of a plane made itself heard once more, and somewhere away to the south-east, on the horizon, a searchlight played on the ragged, rain-filled clouds. The dead-seeming, silent night pressed down like a soft but palpable weight upon the village; nothing stirred in the street, few lights showed. Through the windows of the public house, 'The Cause is Altered', came a faint glow, and a subdued buzz of talk. Immensely tired, feeling somehow deflated and drained of vitality, Reynard sauntered homeward. Suddenly, for no apparent reason, an image flickered through his mind, clear and brilliant as a struck match: he saw again the metal plate on the rear of the Priorsholt bus, with its cryptic inscription which, he found, rather to his surprise, that he was now able to remember perfectly clearly. Simultaneously, another more distant memory recurred: he was listening once more to the announcement made in the gymnasium by the Roman Camp. . . . *'Qualified personnel should report to the recruiting-centre, Department X.19 . . .'*

Reynard stood stock-still for several minutes in the darkened street, his heart beating as though it must burst. Department X.19: the official cypher on the back of the bus, which had struck him at the time as being in some odd way significant, was identical with the code-name of the recruiting-centre. How could he have failed to realize it at the time? And now he remembered something else: it was as though the voice spoke once again – '. . . should report to the recruiting-centre, Department X.19, *not later than 16.30 hours. . . .'*

Mechanically, feeling the futility of his action, he looked at his watch: it was half-past eight. Even supposing he could reach the centre, he would be too late, now: zero-hour had passed, he had missed his chance – his only chance – of escape.

Slowly, possessed by a desolate unhappiness, a sense of remorse which he knew would haunt him for the rest of his life, he walked onward towards the lit windows of his mother's house.

CHAPTER TWELVE

The Patch of Alexanders

During the following weeks, Reynard experienced all the symptoms of one who has suffered some severe emotional shock: he felt unduly tired by any small exertion, and was exhausted by the end of each day; yet he could not sleep at night; he found himself becoming increasingly irritable with his colleagues at the bank, and even with his mother; any small misfortune provoked him to a disproportionate emotional reaction, and to mislay a pencil, or break a match while striking it, was sufficient to bring tears to his eyes. Tiny actions became fraught with a vast, world-shaking significance; to come to any decision, however trivial, was almost an impossibility: even to choose, at lunch-time, between a cup of tea or a cup of coffee, seemed equivalent to a choice between salvation and damnation.

Gradually, however, as the weeks passed, he began to regain his equilibrium. From a doctor whom he visited on the pretext of being 'run-down', he obtained a prescription for Easton's Syrup; he maintained, also, his habit of going for long walks at week-ends; and by Christmas-time he began to feel, at least physically, some improvement.

Christmas passed with, for the Langrish household, the mildest of celebrations; January came, with the first snowdrops in the garden and, in the hedgerows, the first feathering of young green. On his walks, Reynard tended more and more, perhaps from mere lack of enterprise, to take the lane which led past the plantation and over the railway; he did not again, however, penetrate so far as on that first occasion, when he had seen the soldiers at the farm: preferring to turn off to the right, beyond the railway, returning home by a different route.

The plantation at the top of the lane had been fenced in with barbed wire – a fact of which he had been made painfully aware on the night of December the first. The fence – for which there seemed no obvious explanation – was a formidable affair, and difficult to negotiate if one was anxious to trespass on what was now, apparently, private land. Reynard found the wire curiously irritating: not that he was particularly fond of the plantation, but it had become a habit with him to take a short cut through it, and he resented being deprived of the small privilege. It was one of the many trivial set-backs which, in his nervous state, were capable of making him disproportionately angry or unhappy.

One Sunday afternoon early in February, he set out for his walk earlier than usual. The weather was dull and windless; under the hedges, and along the field-borders, streaks of snow lingered from a blizzard of the previous week; and from the trees, still half-frozen, large drops fell heavily, with a sullen reluctance, upon the ice-bound path and the sodden hedgerows.

As he reached the top of the lane, Reynard stopped to look back at the village, which lay directly below him, strung out along the valley: an irregular, extended cluster of red-tiled roofs. At one end was the church-tower, muffled in its surrounding trees; nearby, on its slight eminence, lay his mother's house: bleakly familiar, the rooted centre of this life which he hated, and from which he could never, he supposed, escape.

Skirting the edge of the plantation, he glanced without much curiosity at the steep bank which sloped up from the footpath: here, among the scattered patches of snow, he observed the burnished points of cuckoo-pint pricking the beech-mast, and the barbed, delicate shoots of dog's mercury. He was aware, without any stirring of interest, that the green sprouts showed a slight increase in growth since last week; he was accustomed thus to observe the progress of the seasons, but lately the habit had become purely automatic, and the idea of advancing spring gave him scarcely any genuine, spontaneous pleasure.

At the top of the path, where it curved away round the edge of the copse, was a stile leading into a field. Reynard leaned against it for a moment to rest. As he stood there, the cold, silent afternoon seemed to close in about him, with a sense of confinement; and he was aware of the old process of 'disintegration' beginning, the sense that his mind was dispersing itself, remorselessly and wastefully, towards the circumference of some vast and widening circle. Leaning against the stile, he lit a cigarette. The tobacco, as usual, was tasteless; perhaps he would never, he thought, be able to taste a cigarette again. Resigned to the progressive dulling of his sensibilities, he smoked half of it, and flung the butt-end away. As he did so, he became aware, more acutely than before, of the sense of dissolution within himself; and he experienced a curious and unusual impulse to surrender himself to it. Why struggle to maintain the balance and proportion of a life which he increasingly hated? Any escape, even an escape into nothingness, was preferable. A strange recklessness overcame him: a passionate desire to surrender to every impulse, to throw aside, for once, the self-imposed restrictions which bound him to his diurnal, spiritless routine.

Was it his imagination, or had the afternoon become suddenly darker? This, of course, might be in accordance with the course of nature: dusk fell early in such weather. But it could not be more than half-past three; and now, in February, it should still be light at half-past four or five. Perhaps the clouds had thickened; but whatever the reason, the afternoon did seem undoubtedly darker. The copse lay high on the brink of the valley: but the light, at this moment, resembled the light in some densely forested glen where the sun seldom or never penetrates.

Discounting his impression as a mere fancy, Reynard was about to move onward round the fringe of the plantation. Suddenly he remembered his old, habitual short cut beneath the trees, and was seized by a furious anger against the absurd barricade of barbed wire which deterred him. To-day, he decided, he would go by the short cut; and he began, rather clumsily, to negotiate the fence. It was even more difficult than he had supposed: the wire was ingeniously arranged so that it was almost impossible to grasp the fence at any point. Whoever had erected it had certainly succeeded in discouraging trespassers. Persevering, Reynard did at last succeed in clambering over – at the cost of a long rent in his trousers, another in his coat, and several painful scratches.

A curious elation swept over him, and a feeling of lightness, as though he had unburdened himself of some heavy weight. He moved forward through the plantation, thinking what a pleasant place it was, and how disobliging it was of the owner to close the right of way. Presently he reached the large dug-out, by which he had so often paused, and which he had often been half-minded to enter. Near the entrance, a patch of bright, glossy leaves caught his attention: they seemed to him, in his elated mood, extraordinarily beautiful. He recognized the plant – it was the herb called 'Alexanders'; the precocious, bright green foliage, fresh and appetizing as a spring-salad, was spread over a chalky bank beneath the budding branches of an elder-tree. Knowing the plant to be edible, or at least not poisonous, he picked a succulent leaf-stalk, and rapidly ate it, enjoying with a peculiar relish the green, earthy flavour, somewhat resembling that of celery.

This unconsidered act seemed to release within him some further inhibiting bond; a renewed sense of freedom, of being suddenly relieved from some burden, overwhelmed him. Between the smooth grey beech-boles, he caught a glimpse, far away in the valley, of his mother's house; and knew that his heart had made in that moment a motion of irrevocable surrender.

He turned towards the entrance to the dug-out, which he had always been too lazy or preoccupied to explore. Feeling his old curiosity revive in him, he stepped forward and, without an instant's hesitation, plunged through the crumbling doorway, down a couple of steps, on to the piled beech-leaves within.

CHAPTER THIRTEEN

Buds of Lent-Lilies

The dug-out, when he found himself inside it, was much as he had expected: the floor was buried deep under a drift of leaves, the ceiling almost touched his head. He stood still for a moment, and then noticed, with some surprise, that daylight penetrated *from the other end of the dug-out*. The fact that there were two entrances to the place had previously escaped him; indeed, he could have almost sworn that such was not the case. There was the light, none the less: and it seemed, moreover, to enter at some distance from where he stood, as though the dug-out had been extended to form a passage or covered track.

Curiously, he walked forward towards the light. The floor rose steeply as he approached it: in a moment he would be in the open air again. To his surprise, however, it was several minutes before he reached the source of the light; the passage was evidently a good deal longer than he had supposed.

At last he reached the opening, and stepped rather clumsily out of the dug-out. For a moment, he was seized with a nightmare sense of insecurity, recalling some perilous dream of falling over a precipice. Just as in a dream, the sensation was enough to shock him into complete 'wakefulness' – or at least into an objective awareness of his surroundings. For a few seconds he hardly realized where he was; then, turning to look behind him, he perceived the hump of the dug-out with the beech-trees beyond; between their trunks, he could still catch a reassuring glimpse of the village church and of the high downs beyond.

He realized that he had come out on the opposite side of the plantation: from end to end, the dug-out passage must measure at least fifty yards. It seemed incomprehensible that he should not have noticed the second opening on his previous walks. . . . He strolled on, curiously, along the edge of the plantation, and turned through a gate flanked by tall hedges, into the tract of park-land which lay between the plantation and the railway. But to his astonishment, no sooner had he passed through the gate than he was confronted by a soldier, standing at attention with fixed bayonet, as though about to challenge him.

He stopped dead in his tracks, staring incredulously at the khaki-clad figure before him. The soldier returned his stare: Reynard was aware of small expressionless pig's eyes in a coarse red face.

'Let's see your pass, mate,' said the soldier at last.

Reynard took a step forward.

'My pass?' he said in astonishment.

'That's right, mate.'

'But you can't ask for my pass – I haven't got a pass. I'm a civilian.'

'Them's my orders – all passes to be checked.'

Reynard felt a spasm of pure terror: he paused for a moment, assuring himself that he was awake, and in possession of his faculties. The wintry trees rose calmly against the cold grey sky; a bird twittered in the silence; nothing in the landscape seemed in any way unusual. The soldier, however, stood solidly in front of him, hostile, authoritative, barring his progress.

'But it's absurd,' Reynard protested, speaking with more conviction than he felt. 'You can't challenge a civilian like this on a public footpath, in peace-time.'

'That ain't no business of mine, chum. Let's have your pass.'

At this moment, a corporal walked up to the soldier and exchanged a word or two with him. Reynard had stopped at a few yards distance from the guard, and the words of the two men were thus inaudible to him. He saw the corporal flash him a quick glance, and nod to the other soldier; a moment later, he stepped forward towards Reynard with an air of authority.

'You'd better come along to the guardroom,' he said. He was a heavily built, blond-haired man of about thirty; his manner was brusque and 'official', but not unfriendly.

Reynard stood obstinately where he was.

'I – I don't know what all this means,' he muttered. 'It's ridiculous – you've no right whatever to detain civilians without explanation.'

The corporal's carefully preserved expression of authority relaxed for a moment into a quick, ironic grin.

'No good taking that line, you know,' he said. 'Better come along with me quietly. *I* don't want no fuss.'

Reynard could feel his heart beating with a suffocating violence. For a moment he lowered his eyes, making a supreme effort to collect himself. What was the meaning of this extraordinary challenge? What were the soldiers doing here at all? By what right were they detaining him? Terror swept over him again, and a profound, dimly felt conviction of the inevitability of his position, a feeling that he *ought to know* why this thing had happened. He racked his memory for some clue – his 'training', Roy's curious hints about the 'other lot', his own failure to enlist on December the first. Had he lost his memory? Or was the whole thing an elaborate joke?

'Well, are you coming quietly?' the corporal repeated. 'Or do you want me to call out the picquet?'

There was no mistaking the authority of the man's tone: whatever else it was, the affair was no mere practical joke.

Reynard gathered his faculties together, and met the corporal's eyes again.

'I want to know by what right you're taking me into custody,' he said. But he was aware, even as he spoke, that his voice was curiously lacking in conviction. He cursed the habitual 'nervousness' which prevented him from speaking firmly, authoritatively, as such a situation demanded.

The corporal clicked his tongue, impatiently. 'See here, mate,' he repeated. 'It ain't no good shooting that line. You know as well as I do what the regulations are. It ain't no fun for me, but I've got *my* orders, and it's no bloody good arguing the toss: you'd much better come along quietly, and save trouble for everybody.'

'I've not the least idea what you're talking about,' Reynard replied. Bewildered and exasperated, he strove in vain to speak more firmly; realizing, however, that his voice sounded shrill and frightened, and that the two soldiers were only too well aware of the fact.

The corporal considered a moment: he was evidently slow-witted by nature, but extremely conscientious.

'See here,' he said, his voice taking on a persuasive, almost a kindly tone, 'you'd much better come quietly. . . . I mean it, honest I do. It'll be better for you in the long run.'

'But I tell you,' Reynard burst out, his exasperation causing his voice to rise several semi-tones, 'I've not the faintest idea what you're talking about. Why can't you tell me what's happened – why don't you explain?'

The man's face darkened suddenly: he seemed to draw himself together, preparing for action. His hand reached for a whistle attached by a lanyard to his shoulder.

'You'll know soon enough,' he said, a new note of brutality perceptible in his voice. 'I'll give you one more chance: are you coming along now to the guardroom, or have we got to take you?'

Reynard was silent, his mind swooning into unimaginable abysses. The afternoon seemed suddenly dark: he stumbled, as though some heavy weight had suddenly struck him; and a moment later he felt his arm seized by the corporal. In the same instant he was acutely aware of the smell of the man's body: a faint, bestial taint of dried sweat, tobacco, stale urine. He found himself staggering across the field, the corporal's hand still gripping his arm; aware that, in spite of himself, he had surrendered to some incomprehensible and probably quite unwarranted authority, and that he was already virtually a prisoner.

They progressed slowly across the field, passing beyond a familiar belt of trees; and now, for the first time, Reynard became aware that the broad stretch of chalk pasture, which as recently as last Sunday had been entirely deserted, was now laid out as a military encampment. Bell tents were disposed in orderly rows, Nissen huts had arisen on the further side, near the railway. A fatigue party was engaged in trench-digging; some of the men looked up as the corporal passed with his prisoner and one of them gave Reynard a friendly, complicit wink. The soldiers were stripped to the waist; and their bare arms and shoulders seemed to Reynard to have an oddly incongruous, 'unseasonable' air in the chilly winter afternoon, like precocious buds of lent-lilies springing from the ice-bound soil.

In Reynard's mind a sense of nightmare persisted; yet with each clumsy step forward, the conviction of present reality became stronger. The corporal's grip on his arm, the rank soldier-smell which came off his body, were too real to be the stuff of nightmare; so too, for that matter, were the budding hedges, the scattered lumps of flint strewing the pasture, the patch of red dead-nettle in bloom at the path's edge. He had noticed the patch of dead-nettle on the previous Sunday, and was able to observe now that the plant had advanced into fuller blossom during the intervening week.

It was useless, he decided, to argue further with the corporal; it would be better to wait till he could put his case before a higher authority. Could he, in fact, be suffering from 'loss of memory'? It was a possible and even rather a comforting explanation; yet the events of the last hours, and indeed of the last days and weeks, presented themselves to his mind in perfectly orderly sequence. He was haunted by a sense of intolerable remorse: some defection, some profound and ignoble failure in himself had brought him to this pass. He felt, too, obscurely, that the passage of time had become subtly deranged: it seemed months, years almost, since he had entered the dug-out. Had he perhaps laid himself down on the piled leaves and gone to sleep? It did seem that the distance from one end of the passage to the other had been surprisingly long; yet he had been aware all the time (he was certain on this point) of the light at the other end. . . .

The effort of trying to remember produced in him an intolerable fatigue; he could hardly, he found, put one foot before the other, and he was grateful for the corporal's supporting hand. They were approaching one of the Nissen huts; over the door was painted the word GUARDROOM. A private leaned against the doorway – an old soldier, to judge by the double row of medal-ribbons which adorned his tunic. Something oddly familiar about the figure made Reynard take a second glance; and suddenly he recognized the red face, the sandy hair, the scarred neck: it was Spike Mandeville!

Spike, however, returned his stare without the least sign of recognition, and addressed himself to the corporal.

' 'Ullo, Corp. Got another of 'em, then?'

'Yeah, picked him up by the gate. Is the R.S.M. in his office?'

'Yes, Corp. I just took him in a cup o' char.'

'Okey-doke, then. I'll just wheel this bloke in and get him documented, then you can take him round to the store and fix him up with his kit.'

'Fair enough, Corp.'

Paralysed by fatigue, Reynard could have slept where he was – standing there, unsupported, in the doorway. Had he been given the choice, at that moment, of returning home unmolested or of being given a bed and allowed to sleep, he would, without doubt, have chosen the latter alternative.

'Come on, then, laddie,' the corporal said, leading the way down a short passage. 'And see here,' he added, in a lower tone, 'take my advice, and don't try no bullshit on the sar'nt-major. He won't stand for it, I can tell you that.'

A moment later a door opened, and he was led into a small room furnished as an office. At a table sat a strongly-built, middle-aged man, with keen blue eyes and a small bristly moustache.

'Got another, have you, Corporal? O.K., let's have him.'

The sergeant-major reached for a blank typewritten form from a pile at his side and, his fountain-pen poised ready to write, glanced incuriously at the new arrival.

'Name?' he asked, his voice expressing nothing but a desire to get through a routine job as rapidly as possible.

Seized by a sudden physical nausea, his head spinning, Reynard made a last, supreme effort to collect himself. He was aware of an almost irresistible temptation to give way; to surrender without further protest to an authority for whose just claims he had no proof whatsoever.

'Lost your tongue, or what?' asked the sergeant-major, his pen still poised over the blank form.

Standing unsteadily to attention, Reynard paused, swallowed once or twice, and at last managed to speak.

'I want to know by what right I have been brought here, and for what reason I am being questioned.'

The sergeant-major shot a quick glance at him, then dropped his eyes once more to the desk.

'You'll find it better not to take that line, son,' he said.

Reynard drew a deep breath, aware that his next words would decide the issue: either he must surrender utterly to his fantastic situation, or he must force a passage, as it were, through the barriers of misapprehension and baseless assumption which were rapidly closing in upon him. He must speak out now, or it would be too late: but the more desperately he sought to find words with which to express his indignant incomprehension, the more utterly tongue-tied did he become. The very currency of language seemed to have become inflated: one word seemed of as much value as another, none would express what he wanted to say.

'Look here . . .' he found himself beginning at last, and was shocked at the shrill, unnatural tone of his own voice.

'Well, what is it?' The sergeant-major shot him another impatient glance.

'Look here, I think there's been a mistake — a very serious mistake.'

The sergeant-major laughed briefly.

'No mistake at all, laddie – not on our side, anyway. If anybody's made a mistake, it's yourself.'

'What do you mean?'

'What I say, laddie. You know the present situation: you've only yourself to blame for what's happening to you. Mind you, I think myself you're better off, but the point is you've cut the painter now, so to speak, and you might just as well make the best of it.'

'But I don't understand. . . . You can't just force me to enlist – there's not a war on. *Why don't you explain why you're keeping me here?*'

The sergeant-major gave a cynical grin.

'You ought to know that,' he said.

Reynard paused.

'Listen,' he said, speaking more calmly, 'I want to know why I'm being enlisted against my will. I was going to enlist on the – the first of December. Captain Archer made me sort of promise, or almost promise. . . .'

'*Captain* Archer?' the sergeant-major cut in impatiently. 'Who's Captain Archer?'

'Captain Archer – Roy Archer – he —'

'*Roy* Archer?'

'Yes, he may be Major Archer, now. He said —'

'Look here, laddie, the only Roy Archer I know is Colonel Archer, acting-Area-Commander, and you'd better be careful what you're saying.'

'But he was a friend of mine. He – I mean I did a course of training, it was the new battalion. . . . We were supposed to enlist on December the first, but I was ill, and —'

'Well, you're enlisted now, all right,' the sergeant-major snapped, 'so don't let's have no more of your bullshit about Colonel Archer.'

Again the sense of nightmare descended. Reynard stared back at the plump, weathered face, aware as he did so of the barriers closing in upon him. Through the window the leafless trees rose calmly, immobile in the windless air, against the darkening sky.

'But I don't understand a word you're saying,' he muttered wearily. 'What's happened? Why are you —'

The sergeant-major cut him short, beckoning to the corporal.

'Just get us a copy of that A.C.I. – you know, the Z – oblique – seven – oh – one.'

The corporal stepped over to a cupboard, extracted a printed

form from a file, and handed it across the table. Almost without a
pause, the sergeant-major began to read aloud from the document;
the relevant passage was evidently of some length, and he recited it
rapidly, in a peculiar sing-song voice such as he would have
adopted in reading an oath, or some charge against a defaulter. A
few isolated phrases impinged on Reynard's awareness: something
about 'compulsory registration of non-military personnel . . . units
in occupied territory empowered to enlist or cause to be enlisted
. . . with effect from the first of December . . . emergency regulations . . . services for an unspecified period . . . disciplinary
measures . . .' but of the essential meaning of the whole passage, he
could form no idea whatsoever.

At last the recital came to an end.

'Satisfied?' asked the sergeant-major, looking up with an ironic
grin.

Reynard leaned upon the table for support.

'I – I wish to have an interview with an officer,' he mumbled.
The barriers were closing in; in the darkness of his mind, a single
phrase repeated itself over and over again: *too late . . . too late . . . too
late.* The sergeant-major leaned back in his chair.

'You're at liberty, of course, to ask for an interview with the
company officer,' he said. 'But if I were you I wouldn't bother. I
really wouldn't: it'll do you no good, and ten to one you'll just get a
bollocking for wasting the Army's time.'

'I must insist on having an interview,' Reynard repeated,
speaking with a sudden firmness.

'All right, laddie – but you needn't think you'll get it to-day. I'll
speak to the company officer to-morrow morning. And now we'd
better get on with *this* bloody job.' He lowered his eyes to the form.
'Name?'

Reynard shook his head, forcing words with difficulty from his
parched, contracted throat.

'I refuse – to answer – any questions – till I've been – granted an
interview – with an officer.'

The sergeant-major looked at him narrowly.

'That's final, is it?' he said in a curious tone.

Reynard nodded.

'All right, my lad. I'm sorry for it, but you've brought it on
yourself, you know. . . . All right, corporal – detail two men from
the picquet. No – better make it four. Is the triangle O.K.? Better
warn Private Mandeville while you're about it.'

The sergeant-major suddenly rose to his feet; he was a massively built man, with the torso and the anthropoid stance of a heavy-weight boxer. He looked down at Reynard with an expression which seemed almost pitying.

'I presume you know what you've let yourself in for?' he queried mildly; then, seeing Reynard's blank stare of incomprehension, he added: 'In case you're not aware of it, your attitude makes you liable to disciplinary action under Clause 44 of Paragraph 6B of the Emergency Regulations. Now do you understand?'

Reynard shook his head.

'You don't? All right then – I'll tell you; but I'm afraid it's no bloody good your pleading ignorance. . . .' The man's tone, as he uttered his next words, was curiously tinged with reluctance: as though he were forcing himself, from a sense of duty, to a task which he found personally distasteful. 'Since you don't know,' he continued, 'offenders under this clause are rendered liable to physical correction on a scale not exceeding' – here his voice took on the sing-song, official tone again – 'not exceeding two hundred strokes of the cat-o'-nine-tails.'

Reynard stared back, half-comprehending, at the level, express-ionless eyes.

'You understand now, do you?' the sergeant-major muttered.

Reynard swayed, feeling suddenly sick.

'You can't do it,' he whispered. 'You can't do it – there's no such thing in the British Army – you can't —'

'I'm afraid we can,' the sergeant-major cut in, in a surprisingly quiet, almost an apologetic tone.

At this moment the corporal re-entered the room with four men. They were clad in overcoats, webbing-belts and gaiters, and carried fixed bayonets. As they stamped to attention at the cor-poral's word of command, it seemed to Reynard that the thud of their heavy boots produced an actual physical disintegration in his brain, as though some final strand had snapped, delivering him up at last to a complete anarchy of the spirit. He was overcome, simultaneously, by an extraordinary spasm, a kind or orgasm akin to some degrading and involuntary act of sexuality. The moment passed, leaving him drained of his last reserve of vitality. His head swam, he felt horribly sick. There was a chair near the sergeant-major's table, and he fumbled his way towards it, sitting down so clumsily that he slipped sideways, and fell heavily to the floor.

Assisted to his feet by the corporal, he grasped the chair-back, and once more met the gaze of the sergeant-major, who now regarded him quizzically, with a kind of rueful mockery.

'Well, have you thought better of it?' he asked.

Reynard nodded. 'All right,' he muttered, 'I'll answer your questions now.'

CHAPTER FOURTEEN

Stripped for a Fight

The questionnaire was short, and soon over: name, address, occupation, date of birth, mother's maiden name, address of next-of-kin, and so on. The sergeant-major filled in the last entry with a sigh of relief.

'That's that,' he muttered. 'You've wasted a hell of a lot of my time. . . . All right, Corporal: take him away and get him fixed up. See he gets a good set of webbing – he'll have to parade in belt and gaiters to-morrow. And make sure he gets his injection at the M.I. room at oh-nine-hundred hours. And in case you don't know, laddie,' (turning to Reynard), 'all ranks are confined to barracks for the duration of the Emergency. Right, that's all.'

The next few hours had for Reynard a quality of dream-like inconsequence; he was immensely tired, and must, indeed, for a large part of the time, have been half asleep, performing the necessary actions with a sleep-walker's automatism. He remembered visiting the Q.M.'s store, and being issued with his kit and blankets; later he must have eaten some kind of meal – he recalled the vision of a mess-tin full of some greasy, yellow stew. In due course, he was allotted a bed-cot in one of the Nissen huts, and discovered that the occupant of the next bed was none other than Spike Mandeville.

' 'Llo, cocker,' Spike greeted him, with a breezy geniality. 'Settling in?'

Reynard turned to him.

'Isn't your name Mandeville?' he asked. 'Spike Mandeville?'

Spike nodded complacently, evidently not in the least surprised that Reynard should recognize him.

'That's me,' he replied. 'Spike Mandeville – Spike to me friends.'

Reynard hesitated, not altogether willing to claim an acquaintance which he might afterwards regret.

'I've seen you box,' he said cautiously.

'Oh, ay – that'll be sometime since.'

'It was a few months ago – over at Larchester. I came over with – I was with a friend, who took me to the drill-hall.'

'Ay, the old drill-hall – I know it,' Spike echoed. 'How is the old place? Ain't been there since the battalion was at the depot – must be five years back, now.'

'But I saw you boxing there.'

'Not me, mate. I ain't done no proper fighting for nigh on a coupla years.'

'But I'm sure I saw you. I remember you perfectly.'

Spike shook his head.

'Funny how you can make a mistake,' he said. 'I'd have swore I'd seen *you* before some place, but I can't recall where.'

'In the hut – up on the downs!' Reynard exclaimed eagerly. One might as well, he decided, put one's cards on the table.

Spike looked puzzled.

'Hut? What hut?'

'You know – the hut where we were training – up on the Glamber Downs, by the Roman Camp. You were one of the instructors.'

'Hold it a minute, chum. You're getting me muddled. Glamber you say – oh, ay, I've got you. It must have been when the battalion was there in 'forty-one.'

'No, no – it was only a few months ago.'

'Couldn't have been me – I been up at Catterick till they moved us down 'ere. Mind you, I *did* used to be an instructor – we had a load o' young rookies, and the R.S.M. was keen on boxing, and I used to take on some of 'em in the evenings.'

'That's right,' Reynard said quickly. 'I used to come up with . . .' Suddenly he broke off, feeling that it might be unwise to speak of Roy in public. 'I was in training – I ought to have enlisted on the first of December, but I was ill.'

'Oh, ay?' Spike encouraged, not particularly interested, but evidently disposed to be friendly. 'That's where I must have seen you, then – seems a long time ago, don't it? Nigh on ten years.' He clicked his tongue. 'Ay, it's a long time.'

'But this was just recently,' Reynard insisted.

'Funny how time goes,' Spike continued, hardly aware, it seemed, of Reynard's bewilderment, and soliloquizing purely for his own benefit. 'That war, now – it was six bleedin' years, and when you look back, it seems no more than two or three.'

Baffled, Reynard decided to drop the subject of their previous acquaintance until such time as Spike should be in a mood to listen. The boxer's speech was rather blurred, and Reynard concluded that he had probably been drinking. Nothing else, it seemed, could account for his strange lapses of memory.

Mechanically, Reynard stripped off his civilian clothes and scrambled into the rough Angola shirt and khaki trousers. Next, at Spike's direction, he took his belt and gaiters out to the ablution-room, and addressed himself to the messy task of blancoing them. His fatigue had become, as it were, a pathological condition which he was able to control and, to a certain extent, ignore; he associated it, for no reasonable cause, with the remembered design on Spike's forearm – the snake and the sword. He was not altogether surprised to observe that most of the other men in the barrack-room were tattooed in the same manner.

In spite of his complacent vagueness, Spike was full of offers of assistance, and kept up a flow of friendly but irritatingly consequential chatter to which Reynard found it almost impossible to reply amicably or even, in his state of extreme fatigue, coherently. Later, he thought, he would take Spike into his confidence: Spike, if anybody, would surely be able to explain the fantastic circumstances of his capture and subsequent 'enlistment'.

Meanwhile, squatting on the floor of the ablution-room, he brushed the khaki-green blanco carefully into his new webbing-belt. His sense of the utter helplessness of his position brought him a curious relief; he was back in the Army – that, at least, was a fact; why, and by what extraordinary sequence of events, he had got there, he couldn't begin to understand; but for the present, at least, he would have to make the best of it.

Presently he lay down on his bed, and must have dozed off for an hour or so; when he awoke it was to find Spike sitting once again on the next bed, darning a pair of socks.

'Nice kip, mate?' Spike enquired. 'It's the best place – you can't have too much of it.'

Reynard sat up and, with sudden decision, addressed his neighbour; speaking, however, in lower tones so that the other men in the room should not overhear.

'Look here,' he began, 'you might be able to explain a few things for me. . . .'

'Oh, ay – anything I can do. Got your webbing assembled O.K.?'

'Yes, thanks – it's not that. The fact is – there seems to have been – some extraordinary mistake.'

Spike nodded encouragingly.

'It wouldn't be anything unusual,' he said. 'Not in *this* bleedin' Army.'

'You see,' Reynard went on, 'they brought me in here this afternoon – it was so unexpected – I was out for a walk, only half a mile from here – and – and – well, I was hauled in to the R.S.M. and told that I was back in the Army. It seems so extraordinary – I mean, I had no warning of any kind. . . .'

Reynard broke off, observing that Spike, pre-occupied with his darning, was only half-attentive. He was aware, also, that he was telling his story very clumsily; it seemed almost impossible to find the right words to fit the facts: some curious inhibition weighed upon his mind, making speech itself a difficulty. His vague, halting account must, he knew, sound fantastic and absurdly naive.

'The point is, you see,' he went on, with a vain attempt to make his words sound plausible, 'the point is, the whole thing must be a mistake – they must have picked up the wrong man – probably thought I was a deserter, or something. What do you make of it?'

But Spike seemed now to be scarcely listening at all, and when Reynard repeated, with some impatience, his last words, he looked up with a start of surprise, as if faintly resentful of being disturbed.

Slowly, with an increasing clumsiness, Reynard repeated his story, describing once again his arrest by the corporal and the particulars of his subsequent 'enlistment'.

Spike, now more attentive, did not appear unduly surprised at the account.

'That's right,' he said. 'I saw you come in – I was down by the guardroom. They warned me for the triangle. They've picked up two or three like that in the last day or two.'

'Yes, but *why?*' Reynard exclaimed. 'That's what I want to know. There's no war on – or if there is, it all happened very suddenly. They keep on talking about an "emergency", but no one'll explain what it all means. What *I* want to know is *why, exactly, I'm here at all.*'

Spike shrugged his shoulders and gave a knowing wink.

'That's what we'd all like to know, mate. With things like they are nowadays, how's an ordinary bloke like you or me to make head or —ing tail of 'em? I tell you, mate, I'm fed up with this bloody caper; but it ain't no good complaining – you know that as well as I do, seeing as you're an old soldier. I've had some cribs in my time – I've been up to the —ing orderly room every bloody morning for a month at a time – but where's it got me? Nowhere.'

'Yes, but . . .' Reynard hesitated, and decided to try another line of approach. 'You see,' he began, 'I think I must have had an illness – lost my memory or something – and I seemed to sort of wake up and find myself here.'

Spike nodded, looking sympathetic.

'*I* know,' he said, 'I've felt the same myself. You wake up, like, sort of suddenly, and find they've got you again. Got *me* like that, they did – I'd been in the local on a Saturday night, and next —ing morning, strike me —ing pink if I didn't wake up and find myself in this bleedin' mob. Mind you, I'd made up my mind, like, to sign on again . . . Still, once they've got you again, it makes you wonder how you could be such a B.F.'

Reynard was silent. A dull, despairing sense of futility possessed him; it was useless to argue, to protest, even to ask a straight-forward question. Inevitably, in either case, one came up against the same unyielding barriers of incomprehension or fallacious assumption. One's every word was interpreted in some sense other than that intended: as though people were conversing in some code for which one didn't possess the key; or it was like being in some cave where one's voice gave back, perpetually, the same constant, unvarying echo.

'But look here,' he persisted, hopelessly, yet with an almost hysterical compulsion which he was quite unable to master, 'you remember when you were taking those recruits for instruction –' once again he lowered his voice ' – I used to come up with Captain Archer.'

'Cap'n Archer?' Spike echoed. 'Which one'd that be, I wonder? Not Bill Archer what used to be with us at Gib, was it?'

'This was Roy Archer – he's a major now; at least, the R.S.M. said something about his being colonel . . .'

'Colonel Archer, eh? Area-commander, that's what '*e* is. Pal o' yours in Civvy Street, was he?'

'Not exactly a pal, but. . . .'

' 'Course I remember old Archer,' Spike interrupted. 'Been with him off and on for fifteen years. He's a good bloke, too, if you keep on the right side of him.'

'But don't you remember, at the training-place, when he used to come in. . . .'

'Ay, he was around quite a lot in those days. Good boxer himself, too: I remember a fight he had with a wog, in Alex it was – he fair wiped the floor with him.'

At last Reynard gave it up as hopeless; whether from cunning or sheer stupidity, Spike persisted in evading every question. He seemed incapable of sticking to the point: no matter what the topic, he would find some way to twist it to his own ends, making it a starting-point for one of his interminable reminiscences or for a series of meaningless generalizations about the Army. An old soldier, the Army was for him man's natural element: questions of why or wherefore seemed to him, no doubt, incomprehensible and, as such, not worth bothering about.

Bed-time came at last, and the lights in the billet were switched off. Stripped to his shirt, Reynard crept between the blankets. A young recruit in the next bed leaned over the intervening space to ask for a light, which Reynard provided, at the same time lighting a cigarette himself.

'Settling-in, chum?' the boy enquired in friendly tones.

Reynard hesitated for a second or two, half-inclined to resume, once more, the interrogation which had proved so futile in the case of Spike. He decided, after all, not to repeat the attempt; the boy at his side doubtless accepted the situation without thinking, just as Spike did; and by raising, once again, the question which obsessed him, he would merely run the risk of being considered 'simple' or even insane. Perhaps, indeed, he really was mentally ill; but it seemed important, if so, to conceal the fact. He knew well enough that to appear, in such circumstances, in any way abnormal, would only make his position harder to bear. . . . Moreover, to imagine oneself ill was the first step towards becoming so. At all costs he must *pretend to know why he was here*; for the time being he must accept his position, at least in public; reserving his energies, meanwhile, until such time as an opportunity might offer for stating his case to a higher authority.

He exchanged a few friendly, non-committal words with the boy in the next bed; then stubbed out his cigarette, and was almost immediately asleep.

A vivid and interminable dream made his sleep restless; he was being pursued through a series of underground tunnels which bore a curious resemblance to the disused dug-out in the plantation. Of the identity of his pursuer he remained ignorant: but he was haunted, throughout the dream, by the smell which had exhaled from the body of the corporal who had first taken him under arrest – a faint animal reek of sweat and urine. At a later stage of the dream, he seemed to be standing on a platform in the midst of a vast stadium; he was stripped for a fight, a tight pair of shorts encircling his waist. On the other side of the ring, his opponent crouched in the position of defence: and he recognized, once again, the countenance of Spike Mandeville, who was, at the same time, the tramp with whom he had spent the night in the Nissen hut by the Roman Camp. The beginning of the fight seemed interminably delayed; two individuals in headgear resembling that of Aztec priests were posted on opposite sides of the ring, and seemed to be engaged in a prolonged argument in some unintelligible language. But though their actual words were incomprehensible, Reynard found that he could to some extent follow their argument, rather as one might comprehend the 'drift' of some primitive script by guessing at the pictorial images adumbrated by its crude hieroglyphs.

He woke from the dream with a sense of profound relief that he was not, after all, forced to engage in a boxing-match. Aware of the coarse stuff of the blankets irritating his bare legs, he remembered that he was now re-enlisted in the Army; but in his half-wakeful condition, the fact seemed curiously unimportant. He turned over, and this time slept soundly till a bugle, a yard or two from the open window nearest his bed, blew reveille. Simultaneously, the night orderly sergeant – who happened to be none other than the corporal who had 'arrested' him – flung the door open and stamped heavily down the room between the beds.

'Wakey, wakey!' he shouted. 'Show a leg, there! Come on, you lucky people! Out of it! Let's have you! Parade on the Square in ten minutes – P.T. shorts and shoes, canvas . . . Come on, old soldier –' this to Reynard, who was already sitting up in bed, and had reached for a cigarette. 'You better show these rookies how to get cracking.'

With the rest, Reynard filed out of the hut ten minutes later, clad only in shorts and slippers. A curious exaltation possessed him: he was able, this morning, for the first time for months past, to taste a cigarette. A warm current of physical well-being coursed through him: even the assault of the raw winter morning upon his naked body was in some sense pleasurable. The troops were fallen-in in three ranks on the edge of the plantation; behind them, the bare beech trees were outlined with an icy clarity against a bright cloudless sky. . . . One thought and one only recurred obsessively in the circumscribed field of his consciousness: 'I can taste a cigarette.' The inability to taste tobacco had become so identified, in the past weeks, with the sense of being 'unwell', that the sudden revivification of his palate seemed to him to augur a return to health, a renewal of his basic physical well-being. He realized that, were it not for the irritating lacuna in his memory, which prevented any logical appraisal of his situation, he would be glad to be back in the Army.

The P.T. was strenuous and invigorating. Afterwards, there was a rush to the ablution-room, a good-humoured hustle for wash-basins and latrines. Reynard shaved with difficulty, jostled on either side by his companions. Next came breakfast: a queue at the cookhouse, rashers of fat bacon and spoonfuls of mashed potato dumped unceremoniously in mess-tins still greasy from the last meal. Reynard found that he was extremely hungry: and drinking in quick gulps from a mug of scalding tea, he felt his earlier sense of well-being reassert itself. . . . His personal 'problem', the whole question of his sudden arrest and enlistment, had become isolated, as it were, in a carefully delimited area of his mind; it was no longer the centre of his consciousness, but a territory removed from his immediate apprehension: a fortified position from which he had, for the moment, beaten a strategic retreat, though without any weakening of his intention to make the assault at some future time. . . . His tactics, he quite realized, would have to be carefully planned; most important of all, he must be especially careful *to conceal his ignorance*. Cunning would be necessary: he must at all costs appear to take his position for granted. Only thus, perhaps, could he beat the authorities at their own game. He remembered, with a sudden secret pride, that his totem was the fox.

The next parade was at 8.30, in full marching-order. Aware that his labours of the previous night had at least been adequate, Reynard adjusted the blancoed equipment with a certain pride. Spike was ready with offers of assistance.

' — this for a caper,' he exclaimed. 'But yours don't look so bad – better than some o' these —ing rookies. Wish I'd got time to give me brasses a rub up – but they don't give you a bleedin' chance.'

Adjusting Reynard's shoulder-straps, he muttered confidentially, 'Goin' up before the company officer, ain't you?'

Reynard nodded.

'He ain't a bad bloke,' Spike remarked. 'Hell give you a square deal. But take my advice, mate – don't give him no bullshit.'

After the parade, Reynard approached the orderly sergeant, with a view to requesting an interview with the company officer. A vague, unpleasant memory of his dream of the night before haunted his mind like a bad smell: the sense of being pursued, interminably, down unending corridors by an unknown assailant, whom he would eventually have to engage in single combat – naked, in the midst of an enormous arena, to the accompaniment of an endless dialogue between those two hieratic figures clothed in the panoplied splendour of ancient Mexico.

CHAPTER FIFTEEN

The Image of a Drawn Sword

The orderly sergeant was a regular with twenty-odd years' service; a fat, middle-aged man with close-set eyes, rimless glasses and a thin-lipped, rather cruel mouth.

'Company officer? You won't get no interview to-day – he's away up to Area H.Q. You can come up to-morrow again if you like . . . but if you take *my* advice, you'll drop the whole business. The company officer's a busy man – he ain't got no time to listen to frivolous complaints, see? . . . All right, then – you'd better double round to the M.I. room now, and get your medical. And you ain't had your injection yet, have you?' Consulting, short-sightedly, a nominal roll, he made an entry against Reynard's name. 'Better make sure you get it this morning,' he said, adding mysteriously: 'You'll drop a big bollock if the R.S.M. sees you ain't got yer snake up.'

At the M.I. room, a queue was already assembling. Pressed against his neighbours, Reynard was aware for the first time, with a sickening clarity, of the inescapable crude intimacy with his fellow-men to which he had been subjected by his 'enlistment'. Morbidly sensitive to physical contacts, he found himself now suddenly overcome by a profound loathing of the human body. The scars of an acne, a purulent furuncle, the line of dirt encircling an unwashed neck – these details of the human condition seemed to him magnified, all at once, into a lewd phantasmagoria of squalor. His immediate neighbour – against whose naked flesh his own body was involuntarily pressed – too evidently suffered from halitosis; his trunk and limbs, moreover, were clothed with an abnormal growth of silky black hair, in which Reynard fancied he could detect (though he was possibly mistaken) the 'nits' of *pediculus corporis*.

He waited passively, silent himself, but abnormally receptive to the diffuse, disconnected talk of companions: the old, unchanging Army patter, over-familiar from past experience:

'Roll on pay day.'

'It's a great life if you don't weaken.'

'Some say "Good Old Nobby", and some say. . . .'

' "Dear Mother, it's a bastard." '

' "Dear Son, so are you." '

'Roll on Christmas, and let's have some nuts.'

The queue at length began to move; Reynard's turn came at last. A flurried medical officer pummelled him, auscultated him, tested his urine for albumen, examined his pubic hair for crabs.

'O.K., I'll pass you A.1.,' he snapped, at the end of his examination. It occurred to Reynard to mention that he had been previously invalided out of the Service; but he was aware that the occasion was unpropitious; the medical officer was flustered, over-worked; moreover, he had just passed him as A.1. It would be futile at the moment to put forward any claim to special attention; perhaps later it would be possible to request an appointment with a specialist. Meanwhile, it would be best to wait till he had had his interview with the company officer.

Emerging from his medical inspection, Reynard found that the queue was re-forming for 'injections'. Nobody seemed to know the nature of this particular prophylaxis: probably it would prove to be the routine 'T.A.B.' for overseas drafts, or tetanus anti-toxin. To Reynard's astonishment, however, he perceived, when he approached the front of the queue, that the table at which the so-called 'injections' were to be given was laid out with all the paraphernalia of the tattooist. He observed, moreover, that each man, as he left the table, held out for exhibition, amid sympathetic grins and exclamations, his left forearm, upon which was printed, indelibly and with professional skill, the image of a drawn sword encircled by a writhing serpent.

Feeling slightly sick, yet remembering his determination to make no protest, Reynard submitted to the operation. This was performed by an orderly skilled, it seemed, in the tattooist's art.

'Better than the old identity discs, eh, mate? You won't find it's so easy to desert this time. . . . All right, mate – it won't hurt you: just a prick – now another. . . .'

The process was lengthy and painful; at the end of it Reynard felt faint and sick, and was glad enough to accept Spike's invitation to the canteen for a 'char and a wad'.

'Got your mark all right, eh?' Spike chuckled, observing Reynard's branded forearm. He leaned forward, confidentially: 'Seen orders? I just seen a copy of 'em in the orderly room. . . . They're starting intensive training, w.e.f. to-morrow. . . . Cor, it's a proper shower, that's what it is – just you wait till to-morrow morning, chum. It's going to shake some of these bloody rookies – too bloody true it is. But you and me's all right, mate, eh? We can take it.'

The afternoon was spent in squad-drill and Bren-gun training. Reynard found, rather to his surprise, that he was acquitting himself reasonably well; the drill movements came easily to him, and the gunnery lecture covered familiar ground. At tea-time a sense of warm, relaxed well-being stole over him: he felt almost happy, and even found himself exchanging a few friendly words with a chance companion. The monotonous patois of the Army no longer seemed to him alien and pointless, but pleasant and even rather beautiful – a crude, homespun fabric of friendliness, a basis of possible intimacy. Faces which had previously seemed to him repellent or subhuman were suddenly, in this tolerant mood of after-tea, transfigured; they had become friendly, kind, humorous – even in some cases positively handsome. Reynard was aware, once again, of a curious sense of relief, a perverse and inexplicable joy at his enforced servitude.

Next morning he presented himself once again at the orderly sergeant's office.

'Oh, it's you again, is it?' the myopic corporal queried unsympathetically. 'I thought you was going to be sensible, and let this business drop. It won't do you no good, you know.'

'I'm sorry, I still want an interview,' Reynard said calmly.

'All right, then. You'll have to see the R.S.M. first, though. Hang on outside.'

Obediently Reynard 'hung on' outside for the next hour. The R.S.M., it appeared, was busy. When he did finally appear, and Reynard was marched in before him, the interview was brief and unrewarding.

'You can't see the company officer to-day – he's gone up to H.Q. again. You can ask for an interview again to-morrow if you still want it; but I don't mind telling you you're wasting your time. . . .

All right, Corporal – march him out.'

The new scheme of intensive training started that day. Two hours of rifle-drill were followed by an hour's P.T.; in the afternoon the entire unit was detailed for a cross-country run. At four o'clock there was a parade in full marching-order, at which all equipment was required to be faultlessly blancoed, and the brasses thereon highly polished. Any defect was punishable by two hours' cook-house fatigues and a further inspection at eight o'clock. Reynard was among the unlucky ones; and when bed-time came, after the two hours' 'spud-bashing' and the re-blancoing and re-inspection of his equipment, he could hardly muster the energy to make his bed down and undress. Once between the blankets, he sank instantly into a heavy, dreamless sleep.

Next day the routine of training was renewed: P.T. at 5.30, squad drill till breakfast time: after breakfast, a parade of the entire unit in full marching-order was followed by an hour of gunnery prac-tice, and a further spell of squad drill. Presenting himself once again to the orderly sergeant, Reynard learnt that the company officer was still at Area H.Q.

Next day and the next the training programme was continued, with a progressive increase in intensity. From mere habit Reynard repeated daily his request for an interview: but he began to realize that it was highly improbable that he would ever attain his object. Each day he was fobbed off with some fresh excuse; the morning visit to the orderly sergeant was becoming an almost farcical ritual which even Reynard himself could hardly take seriously. Did it matter so very much, after all, whether he obtained his precious interview or not? The extreme fatigue from which he now con-stantly suffered had induced in him a kind of dull, mindless placidity: he could scarcely remember, now, why he had wanted the interview in the first place, or what he intended to say if and when he obtained it. The day of his 'enlistment' seemed already curiously remote, and the events immediately preceding it had almost lost the quality of reality: only the harsh diurnal routine seemed 'real' to him now. A vague discomfort did persist intermit-tently, a sense of guilt and of some irreparable loss which he couldn't and didn't particularly want to analyse. Rumours of an inspection by the Area-commander in the near future roused in him a faint hope that the 'Colonel Archer' of whom the unit lived in such awe might prove, after all, to be his former friend; but somehow the possibility didn't seem very likely, and in any case would not, probably, make much difference to his situation.

He wrote several letters to his mother, but received no reply. The postal services, it seemed, were badly disorganized by the 'crisis'. He began a letter, too, to a well-off uncle who had been reputed during the war to have important contacts in the War Office. Chronic fatigue made any writing extremely difficult; even the dispatch of a postcard taxed his vitality almost to the point of exhaustion; and the letter to his uncle hung fire indefinitely. He made a number of attempts; but his intention, which was to present his 'case' as briefly and objectively as possible, seemed invariably to become blurred and distorted before he had completed a single paragraph. Re-reading what he had written, he was shocked in every case to observe that some note of hysteria or neurosis had crept in: the tone of the letter was apt to become either abusive or over-obsequious, and too often degenerated, before the end, into a diatribe against the Army or some cringing plea for preferential treatment.

At last one morning his persistence was rewarded: on presenting himself to the orderly sergeant, he learned that the company officer would grant him an interview at nine o'clock.

His first reaction was one of triumph; but as he waited, in his belt and gaiters, outside the company office, he found that his mind had become curiously blank. The interview, so long awaited, had taken on a kind of 'abstract' quality, had become a mere objective to attain which seemed sufficient in itself. The actual statement of his case had seemed the easiest part; he had known by heart – or so he thought – exactly what he should say when the moment came. Yet now, with the critical moment upon him, he found himself confronted with precisely the same difficulty as when he had attempted to write to his uncle; try as he might to rehearse coolly and collectedly what he wanted to say, the words refused to shape themselves to his primary intention. Standing in the corridor, waiting for the sergeant-major's summons, he found himself concocting an extraordinary farrago which, if he ever delivered it, would succeed only in permanently ruining his 'case', and would probably, moreover, result in his being charged with insolence to a superior officer.

At last the sergeant-major beckoned him into the room. He marched forward and came to attention before a long table behind which the company officer was sitting. A fire blazed in the hearth, a bowl of early primroses stood on the table: the room was more comfortable and more 'civilized' than any Reynard had entered since his enlistment.

The officer himself was a short, thick-set young man with a small moustache, and dark hair parted in the middle. Something about his appearance struck Reynard as vaguely familiar. He looked up as Reynard entered and smiled pleasantly.

'Well, Langrish, and what can I do for you?'

Meeting his eyes, Reynard suddenly remembered where they had met before: the company officer was none other than the young man whom Roy had introduced to him in the public-house in Larchester, on the evening of the boxing tournament!

'All right, Sergeant-major, you needn't wait,' said the officer, and the sergeant-major retired. 'Well now,' he said, turning back to Reynard, 'what's the trouble?'

An immense relief flooded through Reynard's mind; the officer plainly didn't recognize him, nor, by the rules of Army etiquette, could he himself claim acquaintance on such slender grounds; none the less, he felt himself to be in the presence of a relatively civilized person who would listen intelligently to his statements, and be able, no doubt, to explain the extraordinary events of the last few days. Reynard saluted smartly: he felt suddenly confident, his mind was clear, the last vestiges of neurosis and hysteria had dropped away from him. He would be able, after all, to state his 'case' coolly and logically, as he had wished to state it in his letters to his uncle.

'Well, sir,' Reynard began, his eyes fixed on the straight central parting in the officer's hair, 'I wish to know – at least, perhaps you can tell me – I mean, why exactly . . .' He hesitated, cursing himself for his sudden loss of confidence. A moment before he had known exactly what he wanted to say: now, suddenly, he was speechless.

'Yes? You want to know. . . ?' The officer spoke with patient kindliness, obviously anxious to help. He seemed prepared, Reynard thought, to devote the whole morning to his problems if necessary. His strong, sun-browned hand played idly with a ruler as he waited for Reynard to speak; the firm, full-lipped mouth was still curled in a half smile.

'Well, sir, the fact is, I consider that I'm here under a misapprehension – I think there's been some mistake.'

The officer looked puzzled: at the same time, Reynard was

aware that his own 'educated' accent had made an impression upon this obviously upper-class young man; and in spite of himself, he felt a faint, rather ignoble satisfaction, half-hoping, in his heart, that even if the officer failed to recognize him, the fact of his gentility might impress him favourably, and even secure for himself some degree of preferential treatment.

'Mistake?' the young man queried. 'What sort of mistake?'

'I don't know, sir. All I know is that I went out one afternoon and – and in the plantation above the village . . .'

'Yes? Go on,' the other encouraged him.

'Something happened – I don't quite know what – I know it sounds silly – but I was just brought in here and – well, I was asked for a pass, and then I was told I was in the Army.'

The officer wrinkled his forehead, and looked at Reynard rather sceptically.

'Are you *quite* sure that you've got it right?' he asked.

'Well, no, sir – it wasn't exactly in the plantation. It was when I came out on the other side.'

'Ah, yes, I get you. But what exactly do you mean – you were *told* you were in the Army?'

'The sergeant-major told me, sir. He showed me some A.C.I. about compulsory enlistment.'

'Well?'

'I didn't understand – I still don't understand, sir – how I could be enlisted without warning, or without receiving an official notification.'

The officer laughed.

'Come, come,' he exclaimed, 'you can't really expect me to believe you'd had no warning.'

'But I hadn't, sir.'

'The Emergency Regulations are perfectly clear.'

'But I'd never heard of any emergency – at least not for the last few months.'

Reynard hesitated, wondering whether to mention his 'training', his association with Roy, his failure to enlist. . . . A sudden weariness overcame him, the whole confused period preceding his 'enlistment' seemed suddenly unreal.

'You say you hadn't heard of the Emergency for some months?' the young man was insisting, with a trace of impatience.

Reynard met his eyes, and felt a pang of fear; it would be better, after all, perhaps, if he told the whole story. For a moment he paused, speechless; then continued, trying hard to speak calmly and plausibly.

'No, sir. I underwent a period – a course of training – I more or less promised Captain Archer that I'd enlist in the new battalion on December the first, but I was ill. Captain Archer did say something about an Emergency, but I gathered it was all rather vague, and more or less a military secret, and – and I. . . .'

Reynard broke off, aware that the officer was regarding him with an incredulous stare.

'Captain Archer? A new battalion? I'm sorry, Langrish, but what you've been saying seems to me sheer nonsense. Can't you explain a little more clearly?'

Reynard resumed, haltingly and confusedly, his strange story, aware that it must sound, to the man seated at the table, fantastically implausible. By repetition, his account had become more or less automatic: he remembered the words he must say, but the actual events which they described had almost ceased to be real even to himself. As he ceased speaking, he realized that the officer was now regarding him with far less favour than before.

'Well, Langrish, I must confess that I'm still totally in the dark as to what you're trying to tell me. I don't know who this Captain Archer may have been – the only officer of that name that I know happens to be the Area-commander, and I presume' (the voice became ironic) 'that you're not claiming acquaintance with *him*. The only thing that seems to emerge is that you *were* aware of a state of Emergency, and I must say I fail to understand what you've come to see me about.'

'But is there a war on, sir, or what?'

The officer stared at him curiously, as though doubting the evidence of his own ears.

'A war?' he chuckled at last, as though the word had amused him. 'I'm afraid you're rather simplifying the issue, aren't you? The conception of war, you know, is rather an old-fashioned one: don't you agree? There's surely not much distinction nowadays between being at war and being at peace.'

'Well, then, sir, is this country under martial law?'

'Martial law?' Again the officer chuckled. 'You're fond of those catch-phrases, aren't you? The trouble is, they don't mean a thing: all law is martial law, nowadays – in fact, it always was. All law, that's to say, is backed ultimately by force. I suppose you'd agree to that? The distinction you make between "martial" law and any other law is just hair-splitting, to my mind.'

Reynard was silent, aware once again of dark incomprehension closing in upon him. Like everyone else, this man proceeded on the fantastically false assumption that the basic facts of the situation *must be known to everybody*. Like the others, he refused – probably indeed he was unable – to state the real nature of the 'Emergency'. Perhaps he just didn't know; perhaps nobody knew; perhaps the whole thing was a vast conspiracy of silence, like the story about the Emperor's new clothes.

Suddenly the officer straightened himself, and laid down the ruler with which he had been fiddling.

'Now, look here, Langrish,' he said, speaking still with a kindly forbearance, but with a certain note of impatience in his voice, 'I don't know what made you ask for this interview; but whatever it was, I think you'll admit that you've put your case very badly. You come to me and spin a vague yarn about a plantation and being asked for a pass and so on and so forth; you then state that you *don't know why you're in the Army*. Now what exactly do you expect or want me to do about it? I'm perfectly ready and willing to do everything in my power to help you, if you're really in trouble. I don't think, moreover, that you're just trying to swing the lead; you seem an educated sort of bloke, and I should say you're too intelligent to attempt anything like that. But can you tell me exactly *what it is you want me to do?*'

Reynard hesitated: it seemed worse than useless to repeat his original question, the immense weight of his fatigue lay heavy on him once more; yet it would, he thought, be futile, having got so far, to let the matter rest here.

'I should like, sir,' he said at last, 'to put the matter before a higher authority.'

For the first time the officer's face underwent a marked change; he flushed angrily, and his mouth tightened dangerously beneath the dark moustache. Reynard noticed, with an alertness born of fear, that his wrists were clothed with a growth of fine, black hair.

'Now look here, Langrish I've been very patient with you, but honestly you'd try the patience of an archangel. What on earth do you suppose you'd gain by going to the Area-commander and asking him *why you are in the Army*? He'd merely think you were dotty. After all, it's not even as if you're a raw recruit – you're old enough to have served in the war, presumably. You weren't a conchy, were you?'

'No, sir.'

'Well, then, I don't see that you've got any admissible grounds for complaint. . . . Anyway, even if you *were* a conchy you'd be unlucky this time – as you probably know, the whole business is washed out under the Emergency Decrees. If you're a conchy, you come under the Class A Defaulter clause, which means you're liable to a hundred strokes of the cat, or, in extreme cases, of what this damfool government calls euthanasia. . . . But that's by the way. What I'm trying to get at is, what the hell do you think you're going to gain by going before the colonel?'

Reynard made no reply: the man was right, it would be useless to demand further interviews, with the colonel or anybody else. A last hope stirred in him.

'I think, sir,' he said quietly, 'I'd better go sick.'

'Go sick?' The officer looked dumbfounded. 'What's the matter with you?'

'That's what I want to find out, sir. I think probably I have some mental illness.'

The officer laughed outright.

'So that's it, is it?' he said. 'You think you can go and tell your troubles to the trick-cyclist? Well, my lad, I'm sorry to say so, but you've had it. If you'd read the Emergency Regulations, as incorporated in Standing Orders – which apparently you haven't troubled to do – you'd know that the Army no longer recognizes the practice of psychotherapy. If you choose to go dotty, you'll be taken into protective custody until such time as you choose to become sane again; if you *don't* choose, then you'll just be kept in protective custody for the duration. And let me tell you, "protective custody" is no bloody picnic. . . . So don't think you're going to wriggle out on mental grounds: it just can't be done nowadays – and I can't say I'm sorry, speaking personally. I always did think psychology and all that was a lot of balls; and I happen to know that Colonel Archer agrees with me.'

As Reynard made no comment, the officer touched a bell on his desk.

'I take it you've nothing else to say?' he asked.

'No, sir.'

'Well, Langrish, my advice to you is to brace up and make the best of it: forget all this nonsense about why you're here, and when-is-a-war-not-a-war, and just try to be a decent soldier.'

Once again his manner was sympathetic and kindly; and in spite of himself Reynard felt a rather ignoble impulse of gratitude towards him. Moreover, futile and inconclusive as the interview had been, he could not help feeling a certain satisfaction in the mere fact of having obtained it.

A moment later the sergeant-major entered, and he was marched out and dismissed. As he passed through the outer office, he encountered the orderly sergeant, who eyed him with a mocking irony.

'Didn't do yourself much good, did you?' he enquired.

Reynard hurried past him, without answering, towards the parade ground. It was true – he hadn't done himself much good; but at least, he thought, he hadn't done himself any positive harm.

CHAPTER SIXTEEN

Tassels of Woodspurge

For the next few days, Reynard continued to derive an entirely illogical satisfaction from the memory of his 'interview'. He had learned nothing from it; his situation was unchanged; yet at least he had attained his object. There was no more he could do; and the knowledge that the whole affair was thus taken, as it were, out of his hands, produced in him a curious, passive contentment. He even ceased to worry, unduly, about the lack of mail; supposing anything were wrong at home, he could, after all, do nothing about it. Plenty of other men on the unit were in the same position. What irked him particularly was the perpetual confinement to barracks; but the rule was strictly enforced, and there were no exceptions. Nobody in the camp, of whatever rank, had yet succeeded in obtaining a pass, even upon the most urgent of compassionate grounds.

As the days passed Reynard found that the extraordinary circumstances of his enforced 'enlistment' had almost ceased to trouble him – had ceased, indeed, even to seem 'extraordinary'. The sense of irresponsibility engendered by his 'interview' had enabled him to shelve the whole business almost completely. Indeed, by the mere fact of ignoring the problem, he began to doubt at last whether it had ever really existed. In public, among his comrades he found it convenient to accept without question, as they did, the fact of the 'Emergency'; and he soon found that, by a kind of auto-suggestion, he was beginning to accept it, with an equal facility, in the privacy of his own mind.

The memory of his civilian life was becoming more and more remote; sometimes, out on a route-march or cross-country run, his attention would be drawn by some familiar landmark, and he would experience a wave of nostalgia. Or, as the lenten season advanced, he would notice some sign of approaching spring: the golden stars of celandines resplendent among their dark, burnished leaves, a clump of early primroses, or the immature reddish tassels of woodspurge. . . . Once, when working with a fatigue-party near the edge of the plantation, he caught a fleeting glimpse of his mother's house below in the valley: it appeared (perhaps owing to some trick of perspective) curiously diminished, as though seen through the wrong end of a telescope.

But such moments of retrospect were infrequent, and soon forgotten; the training-operations, for the most part, took place over an area far removed from the village, which was, of course, strictly out of bounds to all troops.

One of these operations involved a lengthy route-march through the wooded country towards the south-east, and Reynard was haunted throughout the day by an unseizable yet vaguely unpleasant memory. He recalled an interminable afternoon walk – months or perhaps years ago – which had been accompanied by a sense of brooding terror and excitement. But the memory refused to click into focus; that vanished afternoon might have occurred a few weeks before his enlistment, or it could as easily have belonged to his childhood.

The past seemed telescoped into an indistinguishable vagueness; even quite recent events became extraordinarily difficult to 'place'. Only the soldier's life now seemed entirely real. The healthy, stripped existence, free of all responsibility, measurable in terms of a prescribed and simple ritual – there were worse modes of living, Reynard thought. His previous term of service stood him in good stead; and the row of medal-ribbons, which he was ordered to sew upon his tunic, procured for him a certain respect and even some mitigation of the more irksome forms of discipline. He found himself, at last, taking a genuine interest in the diurnal routine; his keenness was doubtless remarked upon; and in due course, he found himself promoted to the rank of lance-corporal.

A few days after Reynard's promotion, it was announced in Part I Orders that the colonel's inspection, rumoured for so long, was to take place during the following week.

'Loads of bull, you see if there ain't,' commented Spike; nor was his prophecy far short of the truth. Two whole days were spent in cleaning and polishing equipment ready for the great day; there were extra parades, extra periods of squad-drill; and the company officer himself addressed the unit, urging upon them the necessity for 'putting up a good show'.

The inspection was timed for three o'clock in the afternoon; by half-past one, the unit was already on parade. The March day was sunny but extremely cold: shivering with the other N.C.O.s in the supernumerary rank, weighed down by the heavy web-equipment, desperately wanting to make water, Reynard waited impatiently for the colonel's appearance. The likelihood of 'Colonel Archer' proving, after all, to be his friend Roy, seemed extremely remote; moreover, even if it were so, it was still highly unlikely that Roy would publicly recognize him. Yet Reynard still cherished, against all reason, a faint hope that an encounter with Roy would in some way alter his situation. The hope was the more unreasonable since, in the light of more recent events, and of the attitude of his superiors, he had actually begun to doubt whether he had ever known Roy at all. Only the Army now seemed truly real, and there were times when the antecedent period – back to and including his previous discharge on medical grounds – seemed to him to have been a mere dream or hallucination. Perhaps he had really been in the Army all the time; perhaps the war was still on. Yet certain details still remained with a perfect and quite undreamlike clarity: the boxing-match at Larchester, the night spent with the 'tramp', the taste of the herb which he had eaten in the plantation.

At last the approach of the colonel was heralded by the re-appearance of the sergeant-major. Presently a group of figures appeared at the far end of the parade-ground; approaching, they resolved themselves into the company officer, the adjutant, a couple of subalterns and a tall figure in a red-banded hat. The parade came to attention, the centre and rear rank were stood at ease; the colonel and his entourage began their round.

Eagerly, Reynard peered between the intervening ranks at the figure of the Area-commander. His view was obstructed, but now and again he could catch a glimpse of the man's face. Was it Roy? An extraordinary indecision afflicted him: staring full at the approaching face, beneath the red-banded hat, he found himself totally unable to make up his mind whether it was indeed his former friend or not!

It was Roy as he might be in middle-age – or possibly it was an elder brother; certainly it was not the jaunty young captain with whom he had run and boxed on the Glamber downs. Yet the nearer the colonel approached to him, the more certain did Reynard feel that it was indeed Roy and no other; and when his own turn came, and the big, heavily built figure paused for a second to inspect his equipment, one glance at the dark, inscrutable eyes was enough: the Area-commander and Reynard's old client at the United Midland were one and the same.

Roy, needless to say, showed no sign of recognition: he passed along the rank with the same aloofness that he used to show when, having cashed his cheque with Ted Garnett, he would walk jauntily past Reynard's compartment towards the doors of the bank. The inspection over, he was wafted away with the other officers to the Mess; the parade was dismissed, and Reynard hurried back to the barrack-room with his companions, anxious to remove his equipment and get a shower before tea.

The episode left Reynard singularly unmoved. Once, perhaps, he had known a man called Roy Archer; possibly that man was the same as the colonel who had just inspected the unit; but it was all so long ago, too much had happened since those far-off evenings at the Roman Camp; it didn't do to think about the past; and after all (Reynard decided) it had never, probably, been very important.

One afternoon Spike Mandeville approached Reynard confidentially.

'See here, Corp.,' he muttered, with a knowing wink, 'have you heard about this dame what comes up to the camp?'

Reynard shook his head.

'Proper old hag, she is, so they say. But she's on the game all right, and does it for love, too. One of the lads was with her last night. She hangs about outside the main gate, by that wood where them dug-outs are – you'd only have to tip the wink to the guard, and bob's your uncle. What say we go and have a dekko, eh?'

Reynard refused; but throughout the afternoon the image evoked by Spike's words haunted him, proliferating like some malignant growth in his mind. Curiously enough, this disturbing image bore no relation to the 'dame' who so obligingly visited the camp, but was associated, perversely, with Spike himself, and more particularly with Spike's scarred neck and cropped sandy hair, these being the details of his friend's appearance which had happened to impress themselves upon Reynard's mind at the moment when he had put forward his lewd suggestion. Later in the day, Spike renewed his proposal:

'Three —ing months it is, since I had a bang,' he said, 'and I ain't too bleedin' particular. Any old bag'll do me – she can't be worse than some of them black bints in Alex, eh? What about it – are you comin' along?'

Reluctantly, Reynard did at last agree; they arranged to meet outside the billet at half-past nine that night. But before the hour agreed upon for their adventure, a circumstance occurred which endowed the whole affair, for Reynard at least, with a far greater importance than it would otherwise have possessed.

The unit mail was distributed at tea-time; and on this particular afternoon Reynard was surprised to receive a large, important-looking envelope, stamped with the letters O.H.M.S. He would have preferred, of course, to receive some more personal communication from the outside world; but even this official missive, whatever it might contain, did at least imply that his existence was still recognized by somebody beyond the bounds of the camp.

Perhaps because he opened it in a hurry, at the mess-table and in public, the contents seemed to him oddly confusing: a bundle of forms of various colours and sizes, pinned together. He examined some of the entries, cursorily: 'Rate of income during the first quarter,' he read, and 'Average figure for tabulated expenses reckoned in inverse ratio (lunar not calendar months)'; and again: 'Spectrum variations (with consolidated totals for financial year beginning March 194–).' Puzzled, he wondered if this documentation really concerned him at all: but there, on the top-most sheet, was a complete duplicate of the questionnaire to which he had replied on his first day in the camp; there were his name, address, profession and other civilian particulars, together with his Army number and the title and location of his present unit. Was it something to do with Income Tax, he wondered? Hardly, for tax was already being deducted from his pay. The name of the military area, printed beneath his unit, suddenly struck him: *Clambercrown Command.* His hand trembled, an extraordinary excitement swept over him, whose source, however, he was quite unable to identify. Then, among a number of blank spaces which presumably required filling in, his eye fell upon the following:

'Disease for which . . . . claims disability allowance . . . .'

In the first blank space (after the word 'which') was inscribed in an unformed clerical hand, the single word MOTHER; and the second space was filled by a long word which, crowded clumsily on to the dotted line, was quite indecipherable. It appeared to begin with 'T' and end with 'sis', and might equally well have been Thrombosis, Tuberculosis or Trypanosomiasis.

The whole document had such an improbable air that Reynard felt inclined to discount its importance. But it so happened that, at this precise moment, he noticed the eyes of one of his companions at the table fixed upon his 'letter' with a gaze of startled recognition.

'You got one of them B-oblique-456-oblique-three-fours, eh?' the young man, a newly enlisted conscript, enquired.

Reynard looked up at the superscription on the top page, and nodded.

'Not bad news, I hope?'

'It looks as if it might be.'

The young man clicked his tongue.

'You can't do — all about it,' he said. 'My missis is dying of T.B. in Nottingham, but the bastards won't even given me a forty-eight.'

Remembering his arrangement with Spike, Reynard resolved to utilize the exploit for another purpose. The guards on the gate could, it seemed, be 'squared', for the purpose of a rendezvous with the unknown *vivandière* from the village, provided one didn't go beyond the boundary-line marked by the beech plantation. It should be easy, though, once out of the gate, to cut through the copse and double down to the village. Getting back would be another matter; but the prospect of future penalties seemed unimportant in the light of more immediate issues.

Faced by the prospect of action, Reynard felt singularly calm and collected; he wondered why he had not braved the sentries before this, and made the attempt to reach home . . . He decided to confide in Spike, with whom, after all, he would have to share the risk of breaking bounds.

Spike, when consulted, proved willing enough to co-operate. He would, himself, 'tip the wink' to the guard on the gate, and if possible keep him in conversation for a few minutes, on the pretext that Reynard was to take first turn with the lady; meanwhile Reynard would have an opportunity to cut off into the wood, and so make his way across the fields to the village.

CHAPTER SEVENTEEN

The Roman Camp

Spike was prompt at the rendezvous: he had spruced himself up for
the occasion, having put on his best battledress, with a brand-new
set of medal ribbons and divisional flashes. His three good-conduct
stripes were carefully blancoed; and he had slicked his short,
smooth hair back with a peculiarly strong-smelling brilliantine. He
greeted Reynard with a self-satisfied grin.

'O.K., mate? Ginger's on the gate – he's a pal of mine, so
everything'll be hunky-dory. You all set? All right, then – let's get
cracking.'

They crossed the camp, and came up to the main gate, which
was open: Ginger, Spike's pal, winked at them non-committally;
nobody else appeared to be in sight. The night was dark and
moonless: nothing could be seen beyond the camp's boundary.

'Go on, chum,' Spike whispered, 'Good luck to you.'

A moment later, Reynard found himself outside the gate. He
skirted the edge of the copse, keeping as close into the trees as
possible. When he had traversed some fifty yards or so, he was
startled to see a tall figure, apparently a woman, moving along the
path ahead of him. If this was indeed Spike's 'dame', she was
behaving in a somewhat unexpected manner; for she appeared to
be hurrying away from the camp as fast as her feet would carry her.

Momentarily unsure of his way (for the night was pitch-dark)
and not unwilling for the woman's company, whoever she might
be, Reynard followed rapidly in her tracks. Soon he found that she
was making for the footpath to the village, and, though his original
plan had been to strike across country, he decided to follow her.

The woman moved quickly, and soon they were approaching the
bottom of the lane, where it entered the village. On the corner

stood the public house 'The Cause is Altered'; apparently the 'Emergency' had imposed no black-out as yet, for the windows were brightly lighted. As the woman entered the radius of light, she suddenly turned about, and Reynard saw, with a curious shock, that her head was heavily veiled with black crape. He paused and they stood for a moment facing one another. Suddenly, with an abrupt movement, she turned away, and hurried round the corner of the public house. Something about her figure, seen at close range, something about the way she moved, struck Reynard as suddenly familiar: he could have sworn (had he not known it to be impossible) that the woman was none other than his own mother.

Knowing that his action was foolhardy, he hurried after her into the village street; as he turned the corner, a light flashed in his eyes, and two khaki-clad figures confronted him.

'210171547 Lance-corporal Langrish?' one of them addressed him, in sing-song official tones.

Reynard assented, dumbly. A second glance had told him that the two men were corporals of the Corps of Military Police.

'That's you, Corporal, is it? Right, I'll have to ask you to come along with us.'

Reynard moved forward. He was not much surprised at the ambush. No doubt, his absence had been discovered sooner than he expected; perhaps the guard-commander had seen him slip out; probably the veiled woman had been employed to act as a decoy. Accustoming himself, at length, to the dim light, he glanced once more at the corporal who had addressed him: and recognized the coarse, red face as that of the 'tramp' with whom he had spent the night in the Nissen hut on the downs.

His first astonishment gave way rapidly to a calm acceptance of the fact; it was not, after all, so very surprising, he thought. The 'tramp' had seemed, at their previous encounter, to know something of the new 'battalion', and of Roy Archer's activities; moreover, he had been already branded with the unit's identity-mark; but doubtless he had had reasons for his reticence. Reynard decided that it would be wiser, in the circumstances, not to claim acquaintance; and the corporal, for his part, betrayed no sign of recognition. Falling in between the two men, Reynard suffered them to lead him, without protest, up the lane towards the camp.

He spent the night in the guardroom. The guards were unobtrusively sympathetic, eyeing him with a certain compassionate awe.

'Cor, you've dropped *your*self properly in the s—,' one of them muttered. 'They've got it in for you, I can tell you – I heard the R.S.M. say they was going to make an example . . . Cor, I wouldn't be in your shoes, chum.'

Only the sergeant of the guard, a coarse-faced, brutal type, regarded him with any marked ill-feeling. Reynard was aware, more than once, of his malevolent glances, and heard him mutter something about 'these —ing conscripts' being 'a load of bum-boys,' and (with a particularly brutal intonation) that he hoped they'd 'spoil his —ing looks for him.'

On his plank-bed, wrapped in a single blanket, Reynard slept the sleep of exhaustion. At reveille he was detailed to scrub the guardroom floor; he was to appear, so he understood, before the company officer at nine o'clock.

'But *he* can't try you,' one of the guards informed him. 'The charge is too serious – breaking bounds counts as desertion now, you know. He'll remand you for the colonel. Glad it's you and not me, mate.'

At nine o'clock he was duly escorted up to the orderly-room, and after an hour's wait on the draughty verandah, was marched in to the company officer. The episode was brief – a mere formality. The guard-commander and the two corporals who had arrested him gave evidence; the company officer, speaking with cold impersonality, warned him that the charge was too serious for him to deal with, and would be referred to the colonel.

Back in the guardroom, he was set to scrub out the adjoining cells; later, under escort, he was sent to the cookhouse to peel potatoes. He performed his tasks with a mindless automatism, aware of nothing more than a slight physical discomfort and fatigue. When meal-times came, he found himself quite unable to eat; though he was grateful, at tea-time, for a mug of scalding tea, and for a cigarette which his escort slipped surreptitiously into his hand.

Once again he slept, exhausted, on his plank bed; the next day passed in an exactly similar manner – scrubbing floors in the morning, 'spud-bashing' in the afternoon. On the following morning he was warned to be properly dressed: he would be coming up for trial before the colonel.

At half-past eight he was hustled into a closed fifteen-hundred-weight truck: the trial was to take place at Area H.Q. The journey, in the dark, jolting truck, had a curiously timeless quality: probably the distance covered was not more than three miles, but to Reynard it seemed that he had been driving for hours when at last the truck pulled up. With his escort, he was hustled across a bare patch of ground to the Area-commander's office. Without much surprise he recognized the Nissen hut where his preliminary 'training' had taken place; beyond lay the earthworks and tumuli of the 'Roman Camp'.

His dull, witless state of mind persisted; recent events were reduced to a confused, meaningless blur, the future was an abyss of impenetrable darkness, haunted by the threat of pain. Afterwards, he could not have said how long he had waited outside the colonel's office; it must have been not less than a couple of hours. At last a warrant-officer made his appearance; prisoner and escort were brought to attention, and marched down a corridor past a succession of offices and departments. Another delay ensued; Reynard was tortured by an excruciating need to make water, but was unwilling to ask permission to do so, lest this should cause more delay. At last, after some twenty minutes' further waiting, the warrant-officer flung open the door, and Reynard, his escort and the various witnesses were marched in.

Behind the table sat Roy Archer – or the man whom Reynard, on a previous occasion, had identified with him; he felt less certain than ever, now, that the Area-commander was, in fact, the 'Roy Archer' who had once (or so he imagined) been his friend.

In a formal voice the colonel read out his regimental particulars and the list of charges; one after another the witnesses gave their evidence: the sergeant of the guard, the two military policemen. The whole procedure remained coldly impersonal; listening to the corporal who had arrested him, and who, a few months since, had stolen his note-case, Reynard experienced a curious sensation of being suspended between two worlds, neither of which seemed to him to have any genuine basis in reality. The present nightmare seemed wholly unreal – at any moment he must surely awake from it; and the past, equally, seemed a dream from which he had awoken, but which haunted him still with its disquieting images: the faces of Roy Archer and of the 'tramp' whose rough bed he had shared, one dark November night, in the very spot where he now stood awaiting his sentence.

At last the interminable procedure drew to its close; the evidence was completed, the colonel rustled the papers before him and, as though aware for the first time of the presence of the prisoner, raised his head and stared Reynard full in the face.

'Have you anything to say?' he asked.

Reynard lowered his head, suddenly unable to meet the dark, searching eyes of the man who might once, in some other world, have been his friend.

'No, sir,' he muttered.

'Will you accept my punishment?'

'Yes, sir.'

The colonel made a faint gesture of satisfaction; shifted his papers, and looked up again at Reynard.

'Well, Corporal Langrish, I'm sorry about this – I gather that you've recently been promoted, and that your record since your enlistment has been exemplary. At the same time, I must impress on you that the charge upon which you've been convicted is an extremely serious one. You're quite aware of the gravity of the present situation; you must have realized that the regulations affecting all ranks at the present time have only been imposed from the gravest necessity. These regulations, I know, have caused a great deal of hardship – I fully realize that. But I'm afraid it's quite unavoidable. We're all in the same boat, and whether we like it or not we've got to put up with it; and it's my job to see that the regulations are enforced.'

There was a pause; then, with a perceptibly harsher note, the voice resumed:

'In your case, Langrish, I'm inclined to be rather less severe with you than the situation merits. I may say that we are empowered to enforce the regulations up to the very limit – and the limit is pretty elastic. In your case, however, in consideration of your conduct sheet, and taking into account that it's your first offence, I am inflicting the minimum penalty which the Act allows.'

Again there was a pause; the next words, when they came, were gabbled so hastily and in such low tones that Reynard could hardly catch them.

'. . . one hundred lashes and fourteen days' field punishment.'

'Prisoner and escort, 'shun! *Left* turn! *Quick* march!'

The warrant-officer's harsh voice, after the quiet, even tones of the colonel, shook Reynard into a sudden apprehension of his surroundings. Following his escort, he turned and marched out; a few minutes later, he found himself, once again, scrambling clumsily into the back of the fifteen-hundredweight. The truck started up, and lurched forward. In the semi-darkness, Reynard

became aware of the voice of his escort:
'... can't send you to the detention-barracks – they're over-
crowded. ... You'll serve your sentence with the unit. ... You
struck lucky, mate – most of the blokes have been gettin' a hundred
and eighty days an' two hundred swipes ...'
    The truck lurched onward, a small moving world of darkness in
the illimitable and deeper darkness of the soul.

The interminable journey was over at last: prisoner and escort
tumbled out, dazed and shaken, on the waste patch of ground
before the guardroom. In the moment of descent, Reynard noticed
with an irrelevant acuteness a trodden clump of foliage at his feet:
the young, lace-like leaves of the plant called Herb-Robert. A brief,
unseizable memory flashed through his mind: darkness and trees,
a widening circle, the sudden fear of dissolution.
    The sergeant of the guard stepped forward, accompanied by a
corporal.
    'Right,' he barked. 'Get inside.' A grin of unconcealed pleasure
transfigured his coarse, bloated face: but for his voice, he might
have been welcoming a long-awaited guest.
    The next few minutes had, for Reynard, the quality of a vivid
and painful hallucination. The momentary vision of the clump of
Herb-Robert lingered in his mind with a peculiar clarity, seeming
more real than the events which were actually taking place. Dimly
he was aware of entering the guardroom, followed by the sergeant,
who kept up a constant, staccato bellow close to his ear: a series of
commands which he found himself obeying with automatic
promptness.
    '*Quick* march! *Mark* time! *At* the double! *At the double*, I said! You
ain't gone —ing deaf, have you? All right, Corporal – double him
along to the cells ... Cor, talk about Fred Karno's Army – you'd
think some o' these bastards was straight out o' —ing primary
school. Cor, just give me a chance, *I'll* show some of 'em what
proper soldierin's like. 'Ere, you – I said "double", didn't I? What
you think you it on —ing tap-dancing, or what?'
    Still at the double, Reynard was escorted to a cell in the
adjoining building. In a few moments, the sergeant reappeared
    'Take yer coat off,' he bawled.
    Reynard fumbled awkwardly with his tunic.
    'Mark time, there! Who told you to stop? At the double!'
    The coat was seized by the corporal and a private, the pockets

emptied, and his personal possessions laid out on the plank-bed.

'Boots off!' bellowed the brutal voice. 'Come on, there – we ain't got all day . . . See there ain't nothing in 'em, Corporal . . . All right, off with yer socks – trousers next. Can't you hear what I'm saying, you —? Drop your pants, I said – you needn't be shy, there ain't no —ing tarts lookin' at you. All right – *mark* time: at the double, I said, didn't I? *Left*, right, *left*, right . . .! Empty his pockets, Corporal . . . *Left*, right, *left*, right . . . Off with yer shirt . . . Who told you to stop markin' time? *Left*, right, *left*, right, *left*, right!'

His face crimson with shame, and panting with exhaustion, Reynard somehow managed to drag off his clothes, at the same time maintaining his clumsy attempts to 'mark time' to the sergeant's command. At last he stood naked, stamping his bare feet still, in double time, on the concrete floor, while the corporal and the private ransacked his pockets and the linings of his coat and trousers for possible contraband. They were in no hurry; nor, in spite of his air of urgency, was the sergeant. Straddled jauntily in the middle of the floor, he regarded Reynard with a broad grin of triumph.

'Go on!' he bellowed. 'Keep it up! Won't do you no harm to do a bit of soldierin' for a change. Lovely, ain't he?' (He turned to the other two.) 'Proper 'igh-class bit o' goods, an' no mistake. Look at 'is skin – lovely and smooth, just like a bleedin' tart's; pity we're goin' to spoil it for you, ain't it?' he bawled, turning on Reynard and advancing a step or two towards him.

The enormous, bloated face swelled suddenly into an engulfing vastness. With a spasm of shame that shook him like some violent rigor, Reynard knew that the last bulwark of his control had fallen; the outraged body took command at last; he was aware of the sergeant turning away in sudden disgust from the brief, ignoble spectacle of his defeat. A tin bucket stood in the corner by the bed: painfully, Reynard tried to crawl towards it; but before he reached it, he fell forward, unconscious, upon the bare dusty floor.

CHAPTER EIGHTEEN

In Some Other World

When he regained consciousness, it was to find himself stretched on the plank-bed, covered by a blanket. He must have slept for some hours, for the cell was in darkness; his head ached unbearably, his mouth was dry; for a moment or two he could not remember where he was or what had happened. Then memory returned; the sergeant's coarse bellowing re-echoed in his ears; he leapt to his feet in sudden panic. The cell, however, appeared to be empty, and the whole building seemed to be strangely quiet. Through the window fell a faint shaft of moonlight: just enough for him to discern the outline of the bed and the corners of the room. He was naked but for his shirt; his jacket and trousers had apparently been removed.

He lay for some time, nervously alert; he was parched with thirst, and at the same time felt an intolerable urge for a cigarette. Presently, a footstep sounded in the corridor; the door opened gently and somebody entered. In the darkness, he was unable to recognize his visitor: but no sooner had he spoken than Reynard recognized the voice of Spike Mandeville.

''Ere you are chum,' Spike muttered, and deposited something on the floor: a moment later, he flashed an electric torch, revealing a mess-tin of greasy soup, a hunk of bread and a mug of water.

Spike made a gesture towards the door, and gave a broad wink.

'The bastards detailed me for guard,' he whispered. 'You know,' he added, one eye on the door, 'I bloody near got copped myself – that bastard O'Reilly was snoopin' round the lines just when you —ed off. There weren't time to give you the wire. He musta recognized you, too, 'cos my mate, Ginger, heard him phone up to the Provost Company and give your particulars.' He eyed Reynard sympathetically. 'I'm sorry it happened, mate – it were just bad luck.' He fumbled in his pocket, and produced two cigarettes and some matches. ''Ere you are, chum – only mind out what you do with the dog-ends. I can't stop or that bastard'll be comin' after me to see what I'm doin'. See you later, chum.'

Spike vanished, closing the door carefully behind him. Reynard drank some water, and tried to eat the bread, but a violent nausea overtook him. Presently he lit one of Spike's cigarettes and lay back again on the bed. The tobacco soothed him miraculously: a delicious sense of well-being stole over him, he felt almost happy. Presently he slept again – for how long he could not tell; when he awoke, the moonlight from the window was somewhat brighter, and he noticed that the mug and mess-tin had been removed.

Clambering from the bed, he padded across to the bucket in the corner; the night air was cold, and he shivered uncontrollably. Hurrying back to bed, his foot struck something with a metallic click; stooping down, he picked up a heavy object which, in the darkness, he could not easily identify. To make certain, he struck one of his precious matches; and to his astonishment, perceived that he was holding in his hand a heavy service-pattern revolver, of the type issued to officers.

He examined the weapon gingerly, and found that it was fully loaded. Bewildered, he forced his fatigued brain to frame some theory which might account for the revolver's presence; perhaps Spike had left it, when he collected the mug and mess-tin; but there seemed no possible reason why he should have done so; and in any case, how could Spike have obtained such a weapon? The fact remained, the revolver must have been placed there by somebody; it had certainly not been there when Reynard entered the cell, nor (he felt certain) at the time of Spike's first visit.

Seeking, with a weary curiosity, for some explanation, Reynard remembered once having heard that, in the German Army, officers charged with some dishonourable offence were sometimes given this kind of opportunity of avoiding trial. Could it be that the revolver had been left with him for such a purpose? And if so, by whom? Suddenly, an odd suspicion crossed his mind: one man only could have been capable of such an action – a man whom he had once believed to be his friend, but by whom he was now unrecognized. Suspicion at last became almost certainty: incredible as it might seem, he was convinced now that the revolver had been

placed in his cell, directly or indirectly, through the agency of Roy
Archer!

Sitting on his bed with the revolver balanced on his knees,
Reynard considered his situation with a curious detachment. He
thought of to-morrow's ordeal: the naked, brutal assault of pain,
the immitigable humiliation which itself was a kind of death; he
thought of the worse humiliations to follow – the hours lashed to a
gun, the futile and interminable fatigues, the obscene jeers of the
sergeant of the guard. . . . He had been offered a means of escape:
why should he not take it?

Cautiously, Reynard took out his one remaining cigarette, and
was about to light a match, when something caught his attention.
Was it his fancy, or had he detected a gleam of light at the closure of
the door? He looked again: narrow as a straw, yet extending from
top to bottom of the doorway, the light was indubitably there.
Silently Reynard stole across the room and very gently, pressed his
fingers against the door: it yielded to his pressure, and swung
slightly open as it had been before. The door was self-locking; once
closed, and he would have lost his only chance of escape.

He sat down on the bed and, lighting the cigarette, considered
his chances. The door at the end of the corridor, usually kept open,
gave on to a waste patch of land behind the guardroom. Beyond
this lay the barbed-wire entanglement which marked the perimeter of the camp; and beyond the barbed wire was the beech
plantation, the path to the village. The distance from the guardroom to the barbed-wire fence was a mere twenty-five yards; at one
point, moreover (Reynard remembered), the wire had been
flattened by the passage of a tank during some recent manoeuvres;
with a running jump, it might be possible to clear it. Everything
depended, of course, on evading the guards who patrolled the
outskirts of the camp. With luck, one might give them the slip; and
once having done so, it might be some time before one's absence
was discovered and the alarm raised.

Reynard's eyes shifted from the revolver to the chink of light and
back again. Finally, he decided to risk it: if one means failed, there
remained the other. . . . It occurred to him, suddenly, to wonder if
the choice were being deliberately offered to him: it was unlikely,
after all, that Spike or any of the other guards would leave the door
ajar accidentally. If Roy had been responsible for the revolver,
might he not equally be responsible for the open door?

Reynard moved softly to the doorway, pushed the door gently

open a few inches, and glanced down the corridor. No guards were in sight; the whole camp might have been deserted, so absolute was the silence. He pushed the door half-open, and padded silently (he was bare-footed, for his boots had been removed with the rest of his kit) down the corridor. As he had expected, the door at the end was open: the chilly night wind, striking his almost-naked body, made him shiver. Clutching his revolver, he glided through the door, and, crouching as low as he could, moved forward across the open ground. Presently he paused, half-screened by a low bush, to reconnoitre: a guard, stationed at the gate, was patrolling the boundary of the camp. Reynard watched his leisurely progress, shivering in the glacial air, and cursing the delay. At length the guard, having reached the limit of his beat, turned back and strolled with a measured step towards the gate.

Now was his chance, Reynard decided; he scuttled, still stooping low, across the remaining few yards of open ground, towards the point where the wire had been flattened. Stopping short a few yards from it, he draped his shirt-tail as high as he could about his waist, clutched the revolver firmly and, drawing a deep breath, took a running jump towards the fence.

An involuntary gasp of pain escaped him as he landed; he had jumped a trifle short, and his right foot and thigh had become entangled with an outlying strand of wire. Trembling with pain, he disengaged himself as rapidly as he could; then, still crouching low, doubled down the path which skirted the plantation. His bare feet made little sound; but the path was rough, strewn with sharp lumps of chalk and trailing brambles, and every step was an agony.

He rounded the corner of the plantation, still unseen; then, abandoning all caution, began to run recklessly down the lane towards the village. Lights glowed still from the public-house at the corner; it could not be so late as he had supposed. It would, he decided, be too dangerous to cross the village street: he paused, thinking quickly, then turned into a field-path on his left. The path led, he remembered, through the orchard below the Rectory: once beyond the glebe-land, and he would be within a few yards of the road leading to his mother's house.

He began to double across the field: the grass felt pleasantly soft to his feet after the rough surface of the lane. Suddenly he stopped, seeing a faint light in front of him; stealing forward, with renewed caution, he perceived a large bell-tent in the corner of the field: the flap was raised and, as he approached, he could see several khaki-clad figures silhouetted against the light within. As he watched, one of the figures moved aside, revealing another seated at a table. The seated man was suddenly clearly visible in the lamplight, and Reynard perceived, with a sinking of the heart, that he wore the red-crowned hat of the Corps of Military Police. As he watched, he saw the man raise his head and stare straight towards him; he flung himself forward upon the grass, and remained motionless for several minutes, watching, in an agony of anxiety, the lighted tent.

The seated figure, however, remained seated; evidently he had not, after all, observed Reynard in the darkness. Reynard turned and, on hands and knees, retraced his path across the field. Regaining the lane, he decided to try another detour, turning this time to the right, down a narrow footpath at the back of some cottage gardens. This would bring him out at the less-frequented end of the village and, if he encountered no further setbacks, he would be able to cross the street, and double back to the opposite end by way of a path through the allotments on the other side.

He moved forward cautiously, holding his hands before him in case of fences or other obstacles. Soon he reached the end of the path and, climbing a fence and crossing the corner of a field, he found himself in the darkened street. Hurrying across it, he turned through a gate leading into a strip of what had once been common-land, and which now consisted of allotments. The tract was bounded at the back by a stream, now dried up, and Reynard decided to keep to the bed of the watercourse, which would afford a certain amount of shelter both from the wind and from possible observers.

The stream-bed was stony and his progress was painful and difficult. Trees and brambles overhung the channel, and by the time he had covered a few yards, his face and chest were badly scratched. He continued along the stream until he encountered a low bridge, crossed by a footway which would lead him back to the village. Climbing on to the bridge, he stood stock-still, listening. A sound reached his ears which set his heart beating: the measured tread of army boots along the village street. Perhaps the military policemen had seen him after all; or it might be merely a routine-patrol. He waited for some minutes, hearing the sound of footsteps gradually retreating. It would be unwise, he concluded, to cross the street as yet; instead, he continued along the river-bed beyond the bridge. The stream, at this point, passed through an orchard belonging to the village carpenter: beyond the orchard lay the lane which led from the village up to the main road. The safest plan, Reynard decided, would be to conceal himself in the orchard, close to the road, and wait until the way seemed clear.

As he stumbled along the stony bed, he noticed that a mist was rising: it was a common enough occurrence in this damp, low-lying valley, and Reynard took little note of it. Soon, however, he observed that the mist was thickening with an unusual rapidity: probably, he thought, it was one of the sudden sea-fogs which often enough drifted inland from the coast, mingling with the river mists, and shrouding the valley in obscurity for days at a time. On the whole, he decided, the fog would be to his advantage: concealing his own movements, and impeding those of his pursuers, who were doubtless less well acquainted with the district than himself.

At last he reached the orchard, and, making his way across it through the thickening fog, came to the lane beyond. A small gate opened on to the roadway: he opened it, and was about to pass through, when a tall figure loomed suddenly into sight, and a light flashed. Reynard retreated, instantly, through the gate: but he realized, with a pang of fear, that he had already been observed. Stepping back among the trees, he remained motionless, aware that the figure with the light had passed through the gate, and was approaching the spot where he stood. Inadvertently, he must have made some slight sound; for the light suddenly swerved towards him, and his pursuer loomed once again out of the shadow.

Reynard instinctively dodged backward; but before he could retreat out of range, a voice hailed him.

'Halt! Who goes there? Advance and be recognized!'

A moment's rapid thinking decided him; if he were to run for it now, his chances would probably be nil; no doubt the orchard was surrounded. He stepped forward; and recognized in the upward glare of the torch the face of the corporal of Military Police who had previously taken him into custody: the 'tramp' with whom, in some remote age and in some other world, he had shared a 'kip' in the Nissen hut on Glamber Downs.

'Oh, so it's you again, is it?' the corporal muttered, as Reynard, holding his revolver carefully out of sight, advanced towards him. The corporal carried a fixed bayonet; as Reynard approached, he saw him shift the rifle from one hand to the other, and fumble rapidly in his breast-pocket from which, a moment later he drew a large police-whistle.

Trembling, yet with a sudden inward calmness, Reynard realized what he must do; the corporal was already raising the whistle
to his lips; at the first blast, the rest of the patrol would be on the
spot, and the game would be up.

With a single bound, Reynard threw himself upon the tall figure,
and, clutching his revolver by the barrel, struck with the butt-end
at the man's face. Taken entirely unawares, the corporal stumbled
and fell; with the speed of desperation, Reynard seized his rifle and,
planting his foot firmly on the man's face, thrust the bayonet home
into the heaving belly. There was a stifled cry, and the big body
rolled over sideways; seizing the fallen revolver, Reynard struck
again, with all his force, at the side of the head; then, grasping the
bayonet with both hands, thrust it again and again into the
yielding flesh, till at last the limbs were still, and the man lay silent
and without a quiver at his feet.

CHAPTER NINETEEN

A Fight to the Death

Reynard waited, squatting at the side of the body, for several minutes; once again he heard the tread of heavy boots passing up the lane and back again; at length the steps retreated along the street, and the silence was unbroken. Evidently the corporal's entry into the orchard had passed unperceived by his colleagues; probably they would assume that he had returned to the police tent in the field by the rectory, and it would be some time, with any luck, before the alarm was raised.

Squatting on the damp ground, Reynard began to be aware, once more, of the cold invading his body. Rapidly, without the least scruple, he proceeded to strip the dead man: unlacing the boots, pulling off the torn, blood-drenched trousers and jacket, and dragging the ill-fitting garments over his own chilled body. He took, also, the corporal's belt and revolver-holster, thrusting his own revolver, for safe keeping, into the front of his tunic. As an afterthought, and by way of completing his disguise, he picked up the red-crowned peaked hat, and crammed it (though it was a size too small for him) upon his own head.

Next, he felt in the trouser pockets and, with a grunt of satisfaction, discovered a packet of cigarettes, a box of matches and a bar of chocolate. He devoured the chocolate greedily; and, carefully masking the flare of the match, lit a cigarette. Crouching by the body, his nerves soothed deliciously by the tobacco, he listened again for any sounds of the pursuit; but the village was plunged in a death-like silence.

Presently he ventured to get up and walk to the gate which led into the lane. This time, he passed through it without incident. He walked slowly, with a measured tread suited to his role, down the lane towards the village. The fog seemed even denser here than in the orchard: he had to pull up quickly, more than once, to prevent himself colliding with the fences on either side.

As he reached the bottom of the lane, he came to a halt; a sudden sound had broken the fog-bound stillness. The noise was distant, but recognizable: the thin, shrill blast of a whistle. It was followed by several repeated blasts, and Reynard fancied that he could hear also a far-off clamour of voices. In the fog it was difficult, almost impossible, to tell from which direction the sounds were coming; they seemed, however, to Reynard's strained hearing, to come from the direction of the camp. Doubtless his absence had been discovered, and the chase was on.

He paused a moment longer, debating whether to make for his mother's house, or to conceal himself nearer at hand. Finally, he turned in through an open gate on the right-hand side of the road: it led, he remembered, to a deserted farmhouse, partly destroyed during the war and never rebuilt.

The mist swirled in ever-thickening clouds through the trees as Reynard made his way up the path towards the house. He had walked for some minutes before it struck him that the path was a great deal longer than he remembered. At last, he realized that he must be on the wrong track; there was no sign of the house. Around him rose what appeared to be a group of tall conifers, in whose shade the darkness seemed more intense than before. The trees were unfamiliar to him; and with a sickening sense of hopelessness he realized that he was completely lost.

For what seemed hours he circled about the strange territory, seeking some familiar landmark, wasting precious matches whose brief flicker revealed nothing, blundering against tree-trunks and barking his shins against a series of unidentifiable obstacles. An immense fatigue began to creep over him; soon, it seemed, he must lie down where he was and sleep: his limbs were no longer obedient to his will, he began to stagger aimlessly, and he could hardly retain his grip on the revolver which, since the raising of the alarm, he had carried ready-cocked in his hand.

The distant whistles and shouts had gradually diminished, and the night was again undisturbed. Presently he struck a narrow path and, following it, came out at last on to what was recognizably a road: the macadam was hard and smooth beneath his feet, and his tread sounded suddenly, dangerously loud.

The road sloped steeply down to the left: following it for some distance, with as light a step as his heavy boots would allow, he at last realized, with a thrill of joy, where he was: the road was that which led to his mother's house. He must have made an enormous detour, rounding the churchyard and a considerable area of woodland, for he had struck the road, as he now realized, at the opposite end from the village, in the neighbourhood of the railway station. A few yards more brought him to the house; the gate was open, and he entered the front garden.

Here, once again, he was struck by something oddly unfamiliar: as he walked up the path, plants and bushes brushed his body, and his steps were impeded by what appeared to be a number of large boulders. Perhaps he had strayed off the path, for the fog here seemed denser than ever, and he found some difficulty in discovering the front door.

The door was unlocked; it was, in fact, ajar – a circumstance which, on a normal occasion, would have surprised him. In his state of extreme fatigue, however, and after the events of the last few days, he was incapable, any longer, of feeling surprise at anything, however improbable or fantastic. He entered the hallway, and felt, automatically, for the light-switch; unable to find it, he struck a match, and stumbled forward into the sitting-room.

The fog seemed to have invaded even the house itself: his brief vision of the room was as clouded and indistinct as the world outside. The match flickered, burning his fingers, and went out. With the final flicker, it seemed that the last spark of awareness in his darkened mind had been extinguished also; he managed to stumble, feebly, to the sofa in the corner and, almost before he could stretch his exhausted limbs upon it, the annihilating weight of his fatigue overcame him finally, and he slept.

It seemed that he had never slept so long; waking to a vague awareness of daylight, he turned over and slept again; rousing once more, after a lapse of many hours, to the darkness of another night. In his waking moments, he was dimly but perpetually aware of the rustling of leaves: they seemed to be blown about the house, in at the windows, around his bed itself. Somewhere, too, the wind seemed to be blowing through living leaves; there was a swaying and creaking as of immense trees, and a sound that was like the threshing of enormous wings. The same dream recurred over and over again, with an extraordinary vividness, throughout his prolonged, intermittent slumber: he was back at the camp (which was indistinguishable from the 'Roman Camp' on Glamber Downs) and engaged in an interminable sparring-match, sometimes with Spike Mandeville, sometimes with Roy Archer himself. But the sparring now, he realized, was more than a mere exercise; it was, in fact, a fight to the death. The fight seemed endless, continuing for round after round; he was conscious of an acute, paralysing fatigue, but some instinctive urge kept him alert, and able to exchange blow for blow with his opponent.

When at length he awoke, it was to experience that profound sense of relief which follows the awakening from a nightmare. He was at home again: the interminable combat on the downs had been a dream. . . . Lying, with eyes still closed, he continued to savour the luxury of his relief; and as the dream-images recurred to him, in reverse order, it seemed to him that the fight with Roy had been only a phase, and a recent one at that, in the progress of his dreaming. The escape, the trial, the whole sequence of events as far back as his enforced 'enlistment' – all seemed blurred, already, into the same dream-texture as the fight on the downs. Layer after layer of remembered experience dropped away from him into the abyss of nightmare. He was at home, the whole fantastic experience had been unreal.

He opened his eyes: a vague, brackish light poured in upon him, but not, as he had expected, through the window of his bedroom. With a rapid adjustment of his perceptions, he realized where he was: the window through which the light entered was that of the sitting-room; he had come in late, and must have fallen asleep on the sofa; once again, he was conscious of an immense relief at having awakened, at last, from the confused, duplicated world of his nightmare.

He shifted his position, which had become uncomfortable, and for the first time became fully aware of his surroundings. A strange dimness filled the room, and he perceived that, beyond the windows, the land lay shrouded in an impenetrable fog. At the same moment, his eyes lighted upon his own uncovered body sprawled on the sofa: and perceived, with a sickening backwash of emotion, that he was clothed in a torn and filthy khaki battle-dress. A sudden, physical nausea racked his body, and for some minutes he remained motionless, as though stricken by paresis. At last, with the trepidation of one who fears to discover, upon his body, the primary lesion of some ignoble malady, he rolled up his left sleeve; and recognized upon his forearm the indelible brand of nightmare – the fanged and terrible serpent coiled about the naked sword.

CHAPTER TWENTY

The Living Moment

For several minutes, or perhaps hours – he could hardly have said which – Reynard lay prostrate and hardly conscious upon the couch. At last he rose unsteadily to his feet: the first object he perceived was the service revolver, which had fallen to the floor. He stooped instantly, and clutched it: standing rigid, for a moment, his ears strained for sounds of the pursuit.

But all was quiet. The fog pressed more densely than ever against the windows; the daylight had a dim, tarnished quality, which might equally have indicated early morning or late afternoon. Gradually, as Reynard stood there, a full awareness of his surroundings impinged upon him; and his sense of nightmare deepened.

The room was indeed his mother's sitting-room: but as it might appear after months or years of neglect, deserted by its inhabitants, and exposed to the slow assault of rain and river-damp, of accumulating dust, or dry-rot and the depredations of vermin. The ceiling dripped moisture, ragged strips of paper peeled from the damp walls; cobwebs, thickened with dust, hung in loops and festoons from every corner. Dust lay everywhere, covering each familiar object with a thick greyish film; the very daylight itself, seeping through the blotched and grimy windows, seemed tainted with the same dead greyness. Upon the rotting mildewed carpet lay a mingled debris of fallen plaster, bird-droppings, dead leaves; one of the window-panes was shattered, and a strand of ivy had penetrated into the room, wreathing its etiolated tentacles about a cheap Victorian statuette of a child nursing a dog.

Reynard stood immobile by the couch, the revolver clutched in his hand; a curious conviction assailed him that he himself was an integral part of the room's desolation: a mere inanimate object, no more significant than the ivy-wreathed statuette; a platform for bird-droppings and the ubiquitous dust. More actual than himself seemed the revolver which remained clasped, by some unconscious reflex, in his hand: it was as though his fingers, like the severed tail of a lizard, retained an independent, disembodied vitality.

The minutes or the hours passed: the passage of time seemed meaningless and incalculable in this fog-bound world . . . The fog pressed against the window, impalpable, amorphous, the very element of nightmare. At last the reflex clutch of his hand upon the gun seemed to flash some signal to his tranced, spell-bound brain; with a somnambulist's stiff precision he moved forward across the room. A detail, hitherto unnoticed, caught his eye: upon the table, thick with dust and scattered with fragments of plaster, were laid out the paraphernalia of a meal – knife and fork, cup and saucer, a plate carefully covered with a cloth. With a mindless, an almost animal curiosity, Reynard pulled aside the square of dust-grimed, damp-spotted linen: revealing a putrefied mess of food – a dried-up fragment of lettuce, a square of mildewed bread, a piece of meat pullulating with maggots. . . . Vaguely, as though apprehending some factual detail of a past age – a tear-bottle, an inscription on a tomb – he realized that the meal must have been laid ready for him by his mother – but how long ago? – against some expected homecoming.

Horror stirred in him afresh: moving still with the unwitting care of the sleepwalker, he crossed the room once more; passed into the hallway and up the stairs. Here, again, the walls and ceiling were falling into dissolution; a tortoiseshell butterfly flapped vainly against the dust-filmed window on the staircase, a small engraving of the sea-front at Glamber bulged damply from its frame of *passe-partout.*

Softly, still clutching his revolver as though he feared a sudden, hostile encounter, Reynard pushed open the door of his mother's bedroom. A current of chilly, fog-laden air struck his face: the window appeared to have been blown inwards by some explosion, and the fragments of glass lay scattered about the floor, mingled with a thin carpet of leaves from the chestnut-tree which grew against the window. A curious odour pervaded the room: a heavy, sweetish taint, recalling the scent of hawthorn-blossom. Upon the bed, a tumbled pile of blankets adumbrated the contours of a human figure. . . . The chill wind stirred the grimy, tattered curtains; as he crossed the room, Reynard caught a brief glimpse of himself in the tarnished mirror: the face of a stranger, an intruder upon some privacy which he had forfeited the right to disturb. . . .

Swiftly, with the furtive motions of a housebreaker, he crossed the room to the bed. With difficulty, he found his voice: his throat was parched, the habit of silence had profoundly inhibited his utterance.

'Mother!' he called. 'It's me – Reynard. I've come home!'

His voice, hoarse and croaking, seemed to defile the frozen, immaculate silence of the room. The covered figure on the bed remained silent, without emotion; Reynard paused, irresolute, unwilling to encounter what he knew, now, to be the worst horror of all. . . . Then, with a quick movement, he pulled aside the coverings, revealing the vestigial form of a human face. Upon the bony framework, the last fragments of putrefying flesh clung precariously, like algae to some tide-washed rock; the eye-sockets were turned upward, meeting his own gaze with a sightless, obscene stare; the mouth lay open, a grinning void of putrescence. . . .

A thunderous knocking below roused Reynard to a sudden awareness of his position. He clutched the revolver and, crossing to the window, which faced the front of the house, peered down, obliquely, in the direction of the front-door; but the fog was as dense as ever, and he could see nothing. The knocking was repeated; half-minded to stay where he was, Reynard hesitated: let them hunt him out, he thought – the game was up, but his two revolvers were still fully loaded. He would at least, he decided, give the redcaps something to think about before they caught him. . . .

The knocking sounded more loudly. Suddenly impatient, and sickened by the heavy odour of putrescence, Reynard moved towards the door; better to get it over, he reflected. They would be sure to shoot back: it would soon be finished. As he walked down the stairs, the obscene jeers of the sergeant of the guard flashed through his mind. He thought of the naked, shameful agony; the rope biting into the soft flesh, pain like the pangs of some monstrous birth, a travail of the spirit. But the men at the door would shoot quickly and shoot straight: it would be better that way.

As he reached the hallway, the knocking was redoubled. Suddenly it ceased, and he heard somebody rattling the door knob: it was strange, he thought, that they hadn't tried it before. A moment later, the door swung open, Reynard levelled his revolver; his hand on the trigger, he saw the tall figure of a soldier, in a peaked cap, dimly silhouetted against the fog. A memory flashed through his mind of another figure, framed in this same doorway, against a bright curtain of rain. . . . Taking aim at the unseen face, he fired. The man plunged heavily forward through the doorway, and fell with a crash, face downwards upon the leaf-strewn floor.

Reynard stood, alert and quivering, waiting for the others. But nobody came. The man must have been alone, after all: the rest were probably scattered about the village, searching other houses. Presently Reynard ventured to move towards the door; with a faint curiosity, he rolled the big body over on to its back, and perceived, with astonishment, that the uniform was that of an officer. He lifted the head, so that the faint light fell upon it; and recognized the face of Roy Archer.

He fell to his knees and, with a sudden passion of tenderness, raised the heavy body from the floor, resting the head against his shoulder. With his free hand, he touched the pallid face, and the crisp yellow hair which he now saw was streaked with grey. Gently he unbuttoned the tunic and shirt, and laid his hand on the warm flesh above the heart. A faint, almost imperceptible pulse throbbed beneath his fingers.

'Roy!' he called, as though across some widening abyss. 'Roy! Don't you know me? For God's sake answer me!' His voice broke into a sob of relief as he saw the lips move faintly. He bent lower so that his face almost touched that of the dying man.

'You've done for me. . . .' The voice was no more than a whisper. 'Not your fault . . . tell them at the camp – tell 'em I said . . . not your fault. . . .' The voice ebbed: but the faint flutter was still there, over the heart. Presently, more faintly still, the lips moved again: '. . . tell them the other lot . . . are moving up . . . from Bladbean . . . they're advancing . . . up by Clambercrown . . . their advance H.Q. is at the old pub . . . the show's on at last . . . and I shan't be there to see it . . .'

Feebly, Roy tried to move his hand; Reynard lifted it, and felt the nerveless fingers close weakly over his own.

'Sorry, old chap . . . I did my best . . . I couldn't have got you less . . . I know it's pretty awful . . . that bloody triangle . . . hurts like hell . . . but you'll come through . . . you're one of us, really . . . I always knew.'

His head dropped back, the faint grasp relaxed. Was it over, Reynard wondered? Suddenly, through the haze of his tears he saw the lips move once again.

'. . . One thing . . .' came the whisper, nearly inaudible now '. . . promise me one thing . . . that you'll go through with it . . .'

Reynard leaned lower, bringing his mouth within an inch of Roy's ear.

'I promise,' he said.

Suddenly a change came over Roy's face; a strangled cough racked him, and a narrow stream of bright blood oozed from his mouth. A violent spasm shook his limbs; then the head fell back, limply, upon Reynard's supporting shoulder. His hand pressed against the warm, naked chest, Reynard remained still for some minutes longer; but the lips were stilled now, the eyes without sight; and the faint fluttering throb beneath Reynard's fingers had ceased at last.

Reynard lowered the body gently, then rose to his feet. He knew now what he must do: his course was clear at last, his native indecision would trouble him no more.

He carried Roy, awkwardly, into the sitting-room, and laid him on the sofa where he had slept: it was a difficult task, for Roy must have weighed not less than fifteen stone. Afterwards he fetched water from the well in the garden (the indoor water-supply appeared to have been cut off) and tenderly washed the pale, bloodstained face; then, pulling down one of the tattered curtains from the window, draped it over the body. Finally, as an afterthought, he picked up the service revolver (he would need it no longer) and placed it, with a last gesture of tenderness, upon the breast of his friend.

Next, he fetched more water and, stripping himself, washed his body clean of the night's foulness. Then, with a last look at the silent figure, he left the house. The fog had lifted slightly: as he walked down the village street, he could discern the faint outlines of the houses. Nobody seemed to be about: no sound disturbed the stillness. Soon he came to the turning by the public house, and began to walk, unhurriedly, up the lane towards the camp. With every step, the air became clearer: by the time he reached the beech-plantation, he had emerged into sunlight. At the corner, where the path turned, he paused, and looked back: the village lay swaddled, still, in mist; only the church-tower and one or two scattered tree-tops showed like floating wreckage above some engulfing flood. As he stood there, Reynard could hear, already, the noises of the camp; and from the same direction, but faint, far off, beyond the wooded downs towards Clambercrown, came the crying of bugles: the 'other lot' moving-up, waiting for zero-hour – the beginning of the 'show'.

The sun fell brightly through the budding beeches; the banks at the sides of the lane were starred with primroses, and the green spears of bluebell leaves pierced the beech mast. A brimstone butterfly fluttered past, and Reynard watched it sail away down the lane in the windless air till at length it was lost to view; engulfed by the white shifting sea which shrouded beneath its merciful folds that ruined house where two bodies lay among the cobwebs and the squalid debris of a world older than time.

Reynard paused a moment longer, filled suddenly with a serene happiness such as he had never known before; his will unflinching, strong in his purpose: aware that past and future were fused at last in the living moment.

He turned, and walked forward with a firm step towards the camp.